Grandma's
MAGICAL
STORYBOOK

This book belongs to:

Grandma's
MAGICAL
STORYBOOK

p^3

This is a P^3 Book
This edition published in 2005

P^3
Queen Street House
4 Queen Street
Bath BA1 1HE, UK

Copyright © Parragon 2002

ISBN 1-40544-075-9

Designed by Katy Rhodes
Language consultant: Betty Root

Printed in Indonesia

Contents

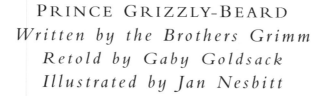

The Frog Prince

Once upon a time, in a land beyond the faraway hills, there lived a little princess. She lived alone with her father, the king. Although she was quite lovely she was also rather spoiled, because the king was a kind-hearted fellow who allowed her to do whatever she pleased, and he gave her whatever she wished.

She had so many toys that she couldn't possibly play with them all. But there was one toy she loved above all else—her golden ball.

One day, the little princess was playing with her golden ball beside an old well in the woods. She laughed and chuckled, as she tossed it into the air and caught it again.

Then she threw it higher and higher, and, SPLASH, it fell down the well.

"Oh, no!" wailed the princess, as she peered into the deep, dark well. "I'll never get it back now. Oh, I'd give anything to get my lovely golden ball back."

Then, as if by magic, an ugly frog appeared on the edge of the well. "What's wrong?" he croaked.

As you can imagine, the little princess was rather surprised to hear the frog talk.

"What did you say?" she asked somewhat rudely, for she didn't like slimy frogs one bit.

"I asked what was wrong," said the frog very politely.

"Not that it's any of your business," said the princess, "but I've lost my golden ball down the well and I'd give anything in the kingdom to get it back."

"Anything?" asked the frog with interest.

"Anything," replied the princess grandly.

"After all, I am the king's daughter. You name it. Jewels, money, land. Anything you want I could give you. But I don't suppose that a slimy old frog could get me my golden ball."

"Oh, but I can," said the frog. "And all I'd want in return is a promise that you will let me eat from your plate and sleep upon your pillow for three nights."

"Yes, of course," said the little princess, secretly crossing her fingers, for she saw no reason for keeping a promise to a slimy frog.

So the frog jumped into the water, and within minutes was back with the golden ball in his mouth.

"Hooray," cried the princess, snatching the ball and racing off before the frog had time for so much as a croak.

"Wait for me," called the frog. "Remember your promise." But it was no use. The spoiled little princess had already forgotten all about him.

12

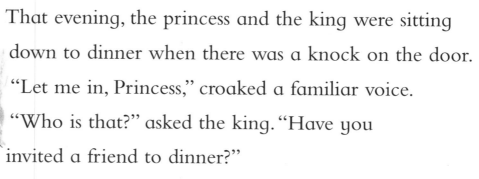

That evening, the princess and the king were sitting down to dinner when there was a knock on the door. "Let me in, Princess," croaked a familiar voice. "Who is that?" asked the king. "Have you invited a friend to dinner?"

And, because she was always truthful to her father, the little princess told him what had happened by the well.

"Then you must let him in," insisted the king. "You have made a promise, and promises must always be kept."

So the princess opened the door, and in hopped the frog. The little princess looked on in horror as the frog made his way across the room and hopped onto the table. "Hmm! This looks good," he said, and began to eat from the princess's plate.

"Yuck! I'm not hungry anymore," said the princess, and she looked away so she didn't have to watch the slimy frog eating her yummy dinner.

13

When bedtime arrived, the princess tried to slip upstairs without her visitor. "Princess, I believe you've forgotten someone," called the king. So the little princess had to come back and take the frog to her bedroom. She placed him on her pillow.

"Yuck!" said the princess, as she climbed into bed with her head close to the frog. She was sure that she would never be able to sleep with an ugly, slimy frog in her bed. Believe it or not, though, in no time at all she was having a really lovely dream about a mysterious prince.

The following evening, the little princess once again shared her plate of food with the frog. This time, she even managed to eat a little herself. And when bedtime came, she carried the frog to her bedroom and wished him good night before falling asleep.

On the third night, the frog came once more. This time, the princess even fed the frog from her golden spoon. Before going to sleep, she read the frog a lovely story. The princess was actually starting to like the frog.

When the princess awoke in the morning she was surprised to find, instead of a frog, a handsome prince gazing down at her.

The prince explained that a wicked witch had changed him into a frog, and sworn that he would remain a frog forever unless a princess allowed him to eat from her plate and sleep on her pillow.

When the king heard the story, he was overjoyed that his daughter had kept her promise and broken the spell. He was even more delighted when the prince asked if he could marry the princess. And the princess? Well, she was delighted that her frog had turned out to be a handsome prince, and promised never to be a nasty, spoiled person ever again.

And so the princess and the frog prince got married and lived happily ever after.

Sophie in Toyland

Sophie was very sad. She couldn't find Peter the Panda anywhere. He was her favorite toy, and she took him to bed every night. It was almost bedtime, and Sophie didn't know how she'd get to sleep without him.

Sophie sat on Beauty, her rocking horse, and rocked sadly back and forth. As her eyes filled with tears, something—she didn't know what—made her rock faster than ever before. She closed her eyes. There was a tremendous whistling in her ears. The next minute, she was tumbling, head over heels, through the air, then floating gently down to land on something soft.

Sophie blinked her eyes. Where was she, exactly?

"Hello, Sophie," growled a voice from above her head.

She opened her eyes and looked up. The legs of a bed—her bed—towered above her. It must have grown! Peeking over the edge of her quilt was Big Ted. Next to him was Little Ted.

"Hello, Sophie," squeaked Little Ted.

Her teddy bears were talking!

Sophie looked around. She was tiny!

"Help," she gulped. "I'm tiny! I've shrunk!" Her eyes filled with tears.

"Hello, Sophie. Welcome to Toyland," called a voice from across the room. It was Samantha, Sophie's doll.

"You're as tall as I am," gasped Sophie. "I'm no bigger than my own doll! What's going on?"

"Don't cry," said Samantha gently. "You're in Toyland, that's all. We're all little here. You'll grow big when Beauty takes you home again."

Sophie turned her head. Beauty, now tiny, just like her, was on the floor beside her.

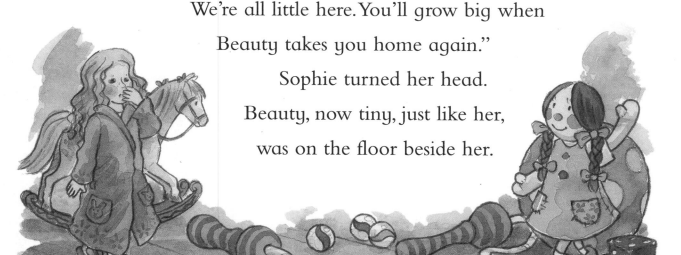

"Look out below!" cried Big Ted.

"We're coming down," squeaked Little Ted.

Big Ted tied one end of a cord to the bed and dropped the other end to the floor. It was the sash of Sophie's bathrobe! The bears climbed down it.

"Let's call the other toys," suggested Samantha. "Wake up, everybody!" she cried.

Suddenly, all of Sophie's toys sprang to life. Sophie's tiniest dolls dashed out of the dollhouse, and the toys that had been put into the toybox jumped down from it.

"Let's play," suggested Big Ted.

"This is fun," said Sophie, as she played games with her toys.

All her dolls and all her teddy bears were there. All of them except Peter the Panda.

"Where's Peter?" asked Sophie suddenly.

They looked everywhere. But Peter the Panda was nowhere to be found.

They gazed at each other in dismay. Then Sophie heard a soft noise. Everyone stood still and listened.

"Someone's calling," said the fairy doll, who had very good hearing.

"It's coming from the top of the bookcase," said Sophie.

They crowded beneath the bookcase. A tiny black-and-white head appeared over the top, high above them. It was Peter the Panda!

"I'm stuck," he squeaked in a tiny voice.

"Gosh!" said Sophie, "I must have put you there when I was told to straighten up my room."

"Please, get me down," begged Peter the Panda.

"But how?" asked Sophie. "The bookcase is so high, and we're so little."

"I know a way," said Big Ted. He ran off and came back pushing Sophie's toy fire engine.

"We can use this," he panted.

"What a good idea!" cried Sophie. She turned the handle on the fire engine's side, and the ladder on top got longer and longer.

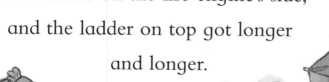

It stretched higher and higher into the air, just the way a real fire engine's ladder does, until the very top of it was resting against the bookcase.

"Now, climb down, Peter," shouted Samantha.

"Ooooh no! I can't!" said Peter.

"Don't worry," said Big Ted. "I'll get him down." He climbed up the ladder and lifted Peter onto his shoulders.

Everybody cheered and clapped when Big Ted carried Peter safely to the ground.

"Thank you!" said Sophie, hugging Big Ted and kissing his cheek.

Just then, the clock on the bedroom wall went "Cuckoo! Cuckoo! Cuckoo! Cuckoo! Cuckoo! Cuckoo! Cuckoo!"

"Uh-oh!" said Sophie. "It's time for bed. I have to go. Bye-bye, toys! Thank you!"

"Goodbye!" shouted the toys. "Please come again!"

Sophie climbed onto the back of her magic rocking horse and began to rock. In an instant she was back in her bedroom, a big girl again.

Big Ted and Little Ted were slumped at the foot of the bed. The fire engine, with Samantha the doll leaning against it, was down on the floor. The rest of the toys were all back in their normal places.

It seemed as though Sophie's adventure in Toyland had never happened, but the sash of her bathrobe was still dangling down the side of the bed. And Peter the Panda was lying safe on Sophie's pillow.

Lucky Sophie had been to Toyland! She'd had a delightful adventure with all her toys, and she'd found Peter the Panda, too. Now she couldn't wait to go to bed and dream all about her wonderful adventure.

Prince Grizzly-Beard

Once upon a time, there was a king who had a beautiful daughter. The king wanted his daughter to marry a prince, and so he invited all the princes from far and wide to try to win her hand. But the princess made fun of all the princes who visited the castle. One she thought too red-faced, and called him "Pinkychops." Another she thought too thin, and called him "Bandylegs." And one, whose beard she disliked, she called "Prince Grizzly-Beard."

"Look at this silly mop," she laughed, tugging the prince's beard. The princess's father was furious. "I've had enough," he declared. "I'm going to marry you off to the very first man who comes to the castle door."

22

The princess thought her father's threat was just a joke and continued to laugh about "Prince Grizzly-Beard" long after all the princes had left. She was still laughing when the first man to come to the castle door turned out to be a ragged beggar.

"What a good joke!" she laughed, when her father told her that she had to marry the beggar. But she stopped laughing when a parson was summoned to conduct the marriage service, and she realized that the king wasn't joking at all.

Before she knew it, the princess was married. "But where shall we live?" she wailed, glaring at the beggar who was now her husband.

"Don't worry," he smiled. "I've got a beautiful hut on the other side of the woods."

"A hut!" wailed the princess. "I can't live in a hut!"

But, because her father said she had no choice, the beautiful princess found herself living in a humble hut. To make matters worse, it lay in the kingdom that belonged to Prince Grizzly-Beard's father.

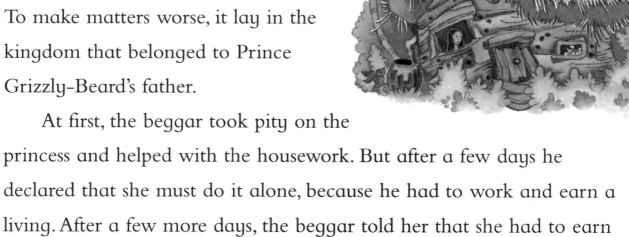

At first, the beggar took pity on the princess and helped with the housework. But after a few days he declared that she must do it alone, because he had to work and earn a living. After a few more days, the beggar told her that she had to earn her keep, and sent her to market with china pots to sell.

The princess had never been so ashamed in her life. She was terrified that someone she knew might see her, and she hid at the back of the market. But even so, the first day's sales went remarkably well, for, on seeing such a beautiful maiden selling pots, lots of people came to buy them.

On the second day, the princess set out her stall in a better position, where more people passed by. But disaster struck when a soldier stumbled over her pots and smashed them all.

When she told her husband what had happened, he was very angry. "I can see that you're not fit for selling pots. Luckily, I've arranged for you to work as a kitchen maid in the king's castle."

So the princess became a kitchen maid, and had to scrub floors and clean lots of very dirty pans.

The princess hadn't been working at the castle very long when the king announced that his son, the prince, was to be married. The castle was decorated with the richest jewels, and the finest food was cooked. As the princess helped prepare for the wedding, she wept.

"To think that I would still be a princess if only I had agreed to marry Prince Grizzly-Beard," she sobbed.

As she was about to leave the castle gate on the day before the wedding, a handsome bearded figure came toward her and took her hand.

He led her into the ballroom. "May I have this dance?" he asked. The poor princess trembled with shame, for she had recognized the handsome figure as Prince Grizzly-Beard. Surely, he had come to tease her.

But he kept hold of her hand and whisked her around the dance floor, much to the amusement of his friends, who thought it was really funny to see the prince making fun of a lowly kitchen maid.

The princess was so ashamed that she wished she could disappear into the floor. But then Prince Grizzly-Beard spoke in a kind voice:

"Fear not," he smiled. "I'm not just dancing with you for fun. Don't you recognize me? I am your husband—the beggar. I disguised myself as a beggar and came to your father's door so that you would have to marry me. I am also the soldier who broke all your pots in the marketplace."

26

"But why have you done all this to me?" cried the princess.

"Because I love you and wanted to cure you of your silly ways. I also wanted to show you how much it hurts to be laughed at by others. But now it is over, and we can have another wedding feast in my father's castle."

The princess was furious, but before very long, she saw that Prince Grizzly-Beard had only been kind so that she would learn not to be too proud and mean to other people.

From that day on, Prince Grizzly-Beard and his princess lived happily ever after. And in time they became king and queen—the kindest king and queen that the kingdom had ever known.

Granny's Magic Closet

Jenna's granny wasn't like other grandmas. She didn't come visiting very often and she never, ever baked cookies or knitted colorful sweaters. Not ever!

You see, Jenna's granny was an explorer. She was always off visiting some faraway corner of the world. So she didn't have time for visiting and baking like ordinary grandmas. But Jenna didn't care. She thought her granny was terrific.

When she did come to stay, she always gave Jenna the most fantastic presents. And she always told the best stories about her adventures.

So you can imagine how excited Jenna was when Granny came to stay for the summer. She couldn't wait to see what wonderful things Granny had brought back with her this time.

But the only thing Granny brought was the biggest, ugliest closet Jenna had ever seen.

"You don't mind me storing it in here, do you?" Granny asked, as it was pushed into Jenna's tiny bedroom.

"But why do you need such a big closet?" asked Jenna.

"Ah, well, things aren't always what they seem," winked Granny. But Jenna wasn't really listening. She was busy thinking how ugly the closet made her room look.

Jenna lay glaring at the closet while Granny told her a bedtime story.

"…and that's how I stopped the Tikuti tribe from burning the closet," finished Granny. But for once, Jenna wasn't listening to Granny. In fact, Jenna wasn't very happy.

Granny had forgotten to bring her a present. And, to make matters worse, she'd cluttered up Jenna's beautiful bedroom with her horrible closet. Granny didn't even have that many clothes.

The next morning, a letter arrived for Granny.

"Fantastic," she said after reading it. "I've been invited to lead an expedition up the Katani River. The only thing is, I have to leave today."

Jenna was very sorry to say goodbye to Granny. And she was even more sorry that she didn't take her awful closet with her.

That night, after Jenna had said good night to Mom and Dad, she sat on her bed staring at the closet. Why did Granny want such an ugly thing? What did she keep in it?

Jenna was sure that Granny wouldn't mind if she took a quick peek. She slipped from the bed and tiptoed over to the closet. Before she even touched it, the door swung open. A soft breeze seemed to come from the closet. Jenna crept closer. Hmm, it smelled lovely—just like a forest.

Jenna stepped in and pushed past one of Granny's old raincoats.

Suddenly she felt herself falling. She closed her eyes and waited for the bump. But she landed on something soft. When she opened her eyes, she blinked twice, then pinched herself. She must be dreaming.

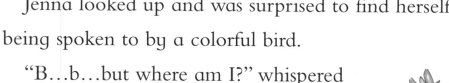

She was no longer inside Granny's closet. Instead, she seemed to be in a beautiful, sunny forest.

"Hiya, Jenna," said a voice. "We've been expecting you."

Jenna looked up and was surprised to find herself being spoken to by a colorful bird.

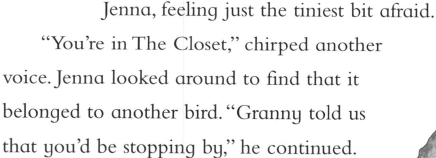

"B…b…but where am I?" whispered Jenna, feeling just the tiniest bit afraid.

"You're in The Closet," chirped another voice. Jenna looked around to find that it belonged to another bird. "Granny told us that you'd be stopping by," he continued.

"B…b…but birds don't talk," stuttered Jenna.

"In The Closet everything speaks," said a tree, helping Jenna to her feet. "That's just the way things are."

Just then, Jenna heard the toot of a horn.

"Look sharp," cried the tree. "His nibs is coming."

Jenna watched in amazement as a funny cart pulled by two rabbits rattled into view.

"Welcome, welcome," cried a voice. And out jumped a little man. The funniest little man Jenna had ever seen. He was no bigger than Jenna was, but his head was just enormous. And on his head he wore what looked like a trash can.

"Ah, I see you're admiring my crown," smiled the funny little man. "It blew in from The World Outside one day. Isn't it the finest crown you've ever seen?"

Jenna tried very hard not to laugh.

"Anyway, allow me to introduce myself. I am Tootiturtletoof, the king of The Closet. But my friends call me Toot for short."

He shook Jenna's hand so hard that her feet almost left the ground.

"As granddaughter of Granny the Great, who saved The Closet from being burned at the hands of the Tikuti tribe, you are an honored guest here. And, since we don't have honored guests every day, we're going to have a party."

Toot clapped his hands and the forest jumped into action. Trees shook their branches, so that fruit and nuts fell onto plates below. Birds dropped berries from the sky. Chattering creatures, carrying trays of cupcakes and sandwiches, appeared out of nowhere. Other creatures danced around decorating the place with colorful flowers and leaves. And glasses of sparkling drinks appeared out of thin air.

"Let the party begin," cried Toot, and a band of squirrels started to play a lively tune.

Toot passed Jenna a glass of foaming soda, and she sat down on a nearby rock.

"Hey, get off!" shouted a voice. "Rocks have feelings too, you know."

Jenna leaped up. "Sorry," she gasped. "I forgot that everything in The Closet can speak."

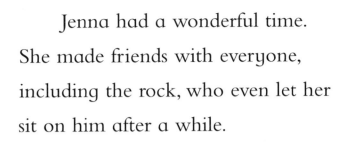

Jenna had a wonderful time. She made friends with everyone, including the rock, who even let her sit on him after a while.

Later in the evening, everyone gathered around to sing a song about how Jenna's granny had saved them from being burned in the Tikuti tribe's fire.

"She's wonderful," said Toot, after they'd finished singing. "She often stops by, and she's even promised to find a safe place for The Closet. A place where somebody will always look after us."

"Let's hear it for Jenna and her granny," shouted Toot. "Hip! Hip! Hooray! Hip! Hip! Hooray!"

"Oooo! I feel a little sleepy," yawned Jenna, a little while later, after she had drunk her third nettle soda and eaten her fourth honey sandwich.

"I think I'll just lie down for a little while." She lay down on a soft bed of grass and closed her eyes. The last thing she remembered was being covered in a blanket of purple leaves by a flock of tiny hummingbirds.

When she awoke, she was no longer in The Closet. She was in her own bed.

"I had the most fantastic dream," she told her mom and dad at breakfast.

"Well it looks like you've been climbing through hedges," laughed Dad, pulling something out of her hair and handing it to her.

Jenna looked down to see what Dad had pulled out of her hair. It was a purple leaf. Jenna tingled with excitement. Her adventure in The Closet must have been real, after all.

"Oh, yes," said Mom. "Granny called last night and said to tell you that you can keep the closet. I can't imagine why you'd want it, though."

"Oh, well, things aren't always what they seem," smiled Jenna. "I will keep it safe forever."

Jenna just couldn't wait to pay her friends in The Closet another visit! And she couldn't wait to tell Granny all about her adventure!

The Wild Swans

There was once a king who had eleven handsome sons and a beautiful daughter called Elly.

Elly and her brothers couldn't have been happier. Their father loved them dearly and gave them everything they wished for.

Then one day, everything changed. The king took a new wife who was wicked and jealous. She was so jealous that she sent Elly to live far away, and turned the eleven princes into wild swans and banished them from the kingdom.

The years passed, and the king sent his wife to bring Elly home. The queen was furious when she saw the princess, for she had grown into a beautiful woman.

The wicked queen was determined that the king should not see Elly's beauty, so she rubbed dirt all over her face and hair.

When the king was presented with this ragamuffin, he would not believe that it was his beloved daughter. Poor Elly was thrown out of the palace, and the wicked queen cackled with glee.

Elly wandered day after day in search of her eleven brothers. The first person she saw was an old woman gathering wood in the forest.

"Have you seen eleven princes?" Elly asked.

"No, my pretty," replied the old woman. "But I did see eleven wild swans wearing golden crowns flying overhead."

Elly continued her search. One day, she came to a beach where she found eleven golden feathers.

"Surely this must be a sign," she thought, remembering the old woman's words. She decided to wait to see what happened.

Elly lay down on a bed
of sand, until the sun began to
set and she heard the flap of
giant wings. Then, suddenly,
eleven white swans landed
on the seashore beside her.

Elly barely had time to
admire their beauty before the
sun sank below the horizon, and the
eleven swans were replaced by eleven handsome princes.

Elly and her eleven brothers were overjoyed to be together once
more. Quickly, the brothers described what the
wicked queen had done to them.

Elly listened to her brothers' tale;
they were doomed to take the
form of swans while the sun was
up, but as soon as the sun set
they became princes once
more. This meant that every
sunset they must be on
land, otherwise they
would fall from the sky
and surely die.

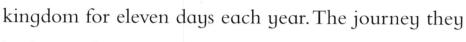

Not only had the wicked queen done
this, but she had also banished them to
an island far across the great sea. They
were only allowed to return to their own
kingdom for eleven days each year. The journey they
had to make to and from the island was long and dangerous.
There was only one tiny island to stop at along the way, so the princes
had to make sure they reached this place before sunset. Otherwise they
would return to their human forms and drop from the sky and drown.

The eleven swan princes were due to return to their
island in the sea the very next day. Elly
begged to go with them, so they
stayed up all night weaving
a mat on which to
carry her.

The next
morning, as the
sun rose, the eleven
swan princes took off, carrying
Elly between them. The swans flew as fast as they could, but because
they were carrying Elly they were slower than usual.

As the sun began to slip beneath the horizon, Elly peered down at the sea and tried not to panic. If they did not reach the tiny island before the sun disappeared, the princes would return to their human form and they would all fall into the angry sea below.

Suddenly Elly spotted a tiny dot below. As the swans circled down, the spot grew larger and larger, until an island appeared. Just as the sun disappeared, the eleven swans vanished, and eleven princes and Elly thumped to the ground. They had made it just in time.

The next morning, they continued their journey. At the end of a long day's flying, they reached their island home.

Elly was delighted with the cave they lived in. She spent each day alone, and each evening she was joined by her eleven brothers. However, she was not happy. How could she be, when her brothers were doomed to spend their days as swans?

Then one night Elly had a dream in which a fairy appeared. She told Elly that if she made eleven shirts out of stinging nettles and threw them over the eleven wild swans, the spell would be broken. But, she added, Elly must not utter a word until the task was finished.

The following morning, Elly got to work. By the time her brothers returned at sunset, she had finished one shirt. But her brothers were worried. Elly's hands were raw from where the nettles had stung her, but she refused to tell them what she was doing.

Day after day, Elly worked on the shirts, until there was only one left to make. She was picking the nettles for the final shirt, when a trumpet sounded and a king rode by.

"What are you doing?" he asked. But Elly could not reply.

When the king stared into Elly's sad eyes, he knew that he wanted her for his bride.

Thinking he was rescuing her, the king carried Elly off to his palace. His servants followed behind carrying Elly's belongings, including the nettles and shirts. At the palace, the king put Elly's things in a tower and gave her a key, so that she could go there at any time.

Shortly afterwards the king married Elly and made her his queen. Elly began to enjoy her new life, but she was still determined to finish the shirts and break the spell over her brothers.

Early one morning, she slipped out of the palace and crept to the tower. Not realizing that her husband was following her, she found the nettles and began making the final shirt.

The king, who was hiding in the shadows, was furious. He was sure that his wife must be a witch. He was just about to jump out and accuse her when he heard the flap of giant wings, and eleven wild swans flew through the window.

He watched in amazement as Elly finished her work and threw a shirt over each of the swans. Then he let out a gasp as the swans vanished and were replaced by eleven princes. The spell was broken.

"What's all this?" cried the king, stepping out of the shadows.

"I can explain," said Elly. And once she started talking, there was no stopping her. Without pausing for breath, she told the king all about the spell her wicked stepmother had cast on her brothers and how she had been making nettle shirts to break it.

The king was delighted that Elly had broken the evil spell over her brothers.

"You must all live with us in the palace," he told the eleven princes. And so they did, until one by one they each found a bride of their own.

Matty and the Narrow Squeak

Matty, Michael, Mary, Martha, and Mac lived with their mother in the Big Barn. Matty was the youngest and quietest of all the mouse children. In fact, he was something of a daydreamer.

One day, Matty sat in a daydream watching a spider spin its web.

"It's not fair," said Michael, the eldest of the five mouse children.

"What's not fair?" sighed Mrs. Mouse.

"It's Matty," said Michael. "He's lazy and useless! He never does any work!"

"The rest of us spend the whole day finding crumbs..." added Mary.

"...and cleaning," said Martha.

"...while Matty spends the whole day doing nothing at all," finished Mac.

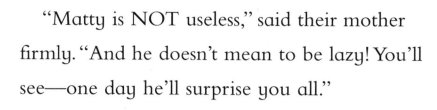

"Matty is NOT useless," said their mother firmly. "And he doesn't mean to be lazy! You'll see—one day he'll surprise you all."

It was true. Matty didn't mean to be lazy. He always meant to do his part. It was just that there were so many things to look at on the farm that he'd forget what he was supposed to be doing. Everything around him, from the largest cow to the tiniest fly, interested him.

On Monday, as usual, the five young mice sneaked into the farmhouse kitchen to find food. While his brothers and sisters scurried about, Matty gazed out the window. Outside, in an apple tree covered in fresh spring blossoms, a mother bird was teaching her babies to fly.

Later, back at home, Mac and Mary unpacked a huge hunk of bread they had found. Martha pulled a big handful of salad leaves from her sack, while Michael hauled in a slice of cheese that was nearly as big as himself.

But Matty had only brought back two very tiny cake crumbs.

"Is that it?" asked Mary.

"That wouldn't feed an ant," sighed Martha.

"Mom won't be pleased!" said Michael, shaking his head sadly.

But their mother wasn't annoyed at all. She just smiled at Matty and ruffled his whiskers lovingly.

Tuesday was cleaning day in the mouse house. Michael, Mac, Martha, and Mary got busy with pans, dusters, and polish, until everything was shining.

Matty was in charge of doing the dishes. But the soap bubbles that rose from the bowl were so beautiful that he found himself gazing dreamily at their rainbow colors instead of doing any washing. As a result, there were no clean dishes when it was time to make dinner.

"Give your brother a hand with the dishes," said Mrs. Mouse to the other little mice.

"Oh, Mom!" complained the four older mice. "It's just not fair!"

But their mother just smiled. "Maybe not," she admitted, "but one day, Matty will show you all."

46

On Wednesday, Michael, Mac, Martha, and Mary gathered grain, while Matty gazed dreamily through the stalks at a particularly beautiful sunset.

On Thursday, Michael, Mac, Martha, and Mary washed every sheet and pillowcase in the mouse house, while Matty admired the distant mountains.

Friday was the mice's day for collecting seeds from the barn. From the door, Matty could see the farmer taking a large basket from the trunk of his car. He stood up on his back legs to see better.

Mac and Michael were having trouble gnawing a hole in a large sack of seeds.

"Matty!" they yelled. "Come and help!"

Matty watched the farmer carefully as he laid the basket on the ground and opened a latch at the front.

"Matty!"

Matty glanced into the barn at his brothers and sisters, then back again at the farmer. The basket, now empty, lay on the ground. The farmer had vanished into the house.

"MATTY!"

Matty turned and looked back into the barn. By now, his brothers had managed to chew a decent-sized hole, and his sisters were collecting the seeds that trickled from the sack like a river.

They were much too busy to notice a shadow falling across the doorway of the barn, or the figure that crept stealthily toward the ladder that led to the loft.

But Matty saw it. And he suddenly knew what had been in that basket.

"It's a cat!" he squealed.

"Run!"

But his brothers and sisters were much too busy to listen. The farmer's new cat crept closer. Its tail twitched as it watched Matty's brothers and sisters helping themselves to grain.

"Run!" squeaked Matty.
This time his brothers and
sisters heard him. They
froze in terror as the
cat sprang.

Suddenly, Matty darted
across the hay, and swiftly whisked
underneath the cat's nose.

He sped down the ladder and out of the
barn. The farmer's cat shot after him.

The cat chased Matty across the barnyard,
twice around the stables, through the pigsty,
and out into the field.

Then, when Matty was sure that the others were safe, he crept
back home to the mouse house.

"You see," said Mrs. Mouse, after she had counted
all her children to make sure they were safe, "I
always said Matty would surprise you one day."

"It was nothing," said
Matty shyly.

But his brothers and
sisters didn't agree—they
thought Matty was a hero.

49

The Tin Soldier

Long ago, in a faraway toy room, there were twenty-five tin soldiers. They all stood at attention in their smart blue-and-white uniforms, and each of them proudly carried a musket (which, as any old soldier will tell you, is an old-fashioned sort of gun) in their arms.

They were all exactly the same, except for one, who only had one leg. You see, he had been the very last to be made, and when they got around to him they had run short of tin; so he only had one leg because there wasn't enough tin for two.

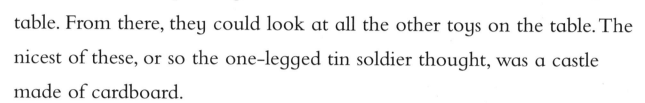

The one-legged tin soldier stood just as firmly on his one leg as his brothers did on two. In fact, some might say even firmer.

When the tin soldiers weren't sleeping in their box, the little boy who owned them would line them up neatly on a table. From there, they could look at all the other toys on the table. The nicest of these, or so the one-legged tin soldier thought, was a castle made of cardboard.

The one-legged tin soldier spent hours gazing at that castle. He knew every little tree and creature that surrounded it. He thought they were lovely, but the loveliest of them all was a tiny lady who stood in a doorway. Though the tin soldier didn't know it, the lady was a dancer. She was dressed in a beautiful lace dress, and wore a red rose, made from a tiny piece of tin, in her hair. She stretched out both arms, and held one leg so high in the air, the way dancers can, that the one-legged tin soldier couldn't see it. Because of this, he thought she only had one leg, just like him.

"She'd make me a perfect wife," thought the tin soldier. "But she's much too grand. After all, she lives in a splendid castle, while I only have a box to call home. And I have to share that with my twenty-four brothers. But I'd like to speak to her, anyway."

So the one-legged tin soldier hid behind a Jack-in-the-box that stood on the table, and kept quiet.

Later that night, when all the other tin soldiers had been put away, and the people of the house had gone to bed, the toys blinked their eyes, stretched their arms and legs, and began to play.

The other tin soldiers rattled in their box and shouted angrily because they couldn't open the locked lid. The clockwork mouse raced across the table, the spinning top spun, and the toy train whizzed around and around on its track.

The only toys that didn't move were the dancer and the one-legged tin soldier. The dancer just stood there with her arms high in the air, and the tin soldier just stood at attention as he stared at her.

At midnight the clock struck twelve, and the lid of the Jack-in-the-box, behind which the tin soldier was hiding, flew open. All the toys knew that the Jack-in-the-box was something of an evil magician.

"Don't you know that staring is rude," the Jack-in-the-box shouted at the tin soldier. But the tin soldier was not scared, and paid no attention. He clung to his musket and stood at attention.

"You just wait until tomorrow," said the Jack-in-the-box, before springing back into his box.

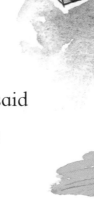

The next morning, when the maid was cleaning the toy room, the one-legged tin soldier was put on the windowsill out of the way. And there he stood at attention, until a gust of wind blew him out the window. It could have been an accident, but the tin soldier couldn't help thinking that the Jack-in-the-box had worked some sort of magic.

It was a long way to the sidewalk below, and the tin soldier landed with quite a bump. But, being a brave soldier, he didn't make a sound. He just clung to his musket and stood at attention, even though it had started to rain.

It rained so hard that the gutters of the streets began to fill with water. Eventually, though, it stopped raining and some children came out to play.

"Wow, look! A tin soldier," said a little girl. "Let's make him a boat and send him sailing down the gutter."

So the tin soldier found himself afloat in a boat made of newspaper. The boat rocked and swayed as it made its way along the gutter, but the tin soldier never stopped standing at attention, even when the boat whirled down a dark sewer pipe.

"What's going to happen to me now?" thought the soldier. "It's all that Jack-in-the-box's fault. If only I had that one-legged lady with me, I wouldn't be so afraid of the dark."

At that moment, the tin soldier heard a rustle and a scratch, and a big, ugly water rat jumped out of a hole in the side of the sewer. "Passport please!" shouted the water rat.

But the tin soldier said nothing and sailed on. The water rat followed him. "Stop that soldier!" he cried. "He has not shown his passport. I don't even think he has one!" But no one paid any attention, and the water rat was unable to keep up with the paper boat.

The tin soldier was swept on and on. Soon he could see daylight at the end of the tunnel. Then he heard a roaring sound, and before he could blink he was swept into a powerful waterfall. The boat spun round and round as it was washed into a canal below. But the tin soldier never cried out, for soldiers did not do such things.

The tin soldier stood at attention as the paper boat began to sink. Soon he was up to his neck in water, but he still stood at attention. Then the boat split in two and the tin soldier sank down through the water. The tin soldier felt sure that he was going to drown and wished that the little dancer were with him.

Then, all of a sudden, GULP, the tin soldier was swallowed by a large fish. It was even darker inside the fish than it had been in the sewer. And it was narrower, too. Once more, the tin soldier wished that the dancer were by his side.

The fish swam up and down for what seemed like ages. Then, suddenly, it began wriggling this way and that. Then, just as suddenly, it became very still.

GULP!

The tin soldier stood at attention and wondered what was happening in this dark, dark place. He heard a strange swishing sound, and the next moment it wasn't dark anymore; daylight was shining down onto him.

"Hey, it's the tin soldier," cried a familiar voice. It was the maid who had put him on the windowsill earlier that morning. You see, the fish had been caught in the canal and taken to market, where the maid had bought him and carried him home. Now that the fish had been cut open by a large kitchen knife, the tin soldier was free once more.

After he'd been washed, the tin soldier was taken back to the toy room and stood beside his toy soldier brothers on the table.

Everything was just as it had been before he left. How the children laughed and marveled when they heard how the one-legged tin soldier had arrived back home in the tummy of the fish.

Everyone was pleased to see the tin soldier again. Everybody, that is, except for the Jack-in-the-box, whom the children were playing with. Every time one of the children opened his lid, he sprang out and glared at the tin soldier, as if to say, "Just you wait." But the tin soldier was not scared of the Jack-in-the-box's magic.

He stood at attention and felt his heart lift as he saw that the dancer was standing in exactly the same place as before. He looked at her, and she looked at him, but neither of them said a word.

Suddenly, a gust of wind came through the window and blew the one-legged tin soldier from the table into the fire. "It's sure to be the Jack-in-the-box's doing," thought the tin soldier, as the flames melted his blue-and-white uniform. Then he started to bend as the fire melted his body.

A door opened, and the breeze caught hold of the tiny paper dancer and blew her straight into the fire too.

The one-legged tin soldier and the dancer stared at each other for one last time as they both disappeared in the flames.

When the maid cleaned out the fire the next morning, she was surprised to find something nestling among the ashes. The tin soldier had melted into the shape of a little tin heart, and the red tin rose, from the hair of the little dancer, was stuck firmly to it. The maid carefully placed the little heart with the red rose on the mantelpiece, where it stayed for many years to come. The one-legged tin soldier and the dancer were together at last!

The Worthless Witch

Hazel wasn't really what you'd call a great witch. She had all the right stuff—a big pointy black hat, a swirling cloak, and a long broomstick covered with cobwebs. She even had her very own black cat called Mouser. The problem was that Hazel just wasn't very good at magic spells anymore.

A long time ago, when Hazel was fresh from magic school, she had been the whizziest witch in the neighborhood. She could whip up a magic potion in a jiffy, and her secret recipe for laughing powder was the envy of every witch for miles around.

There was always someone on her doorstep wanting help with something —a lotion for curing boils, a love potion, or a spell to make the sun come out. But these days, there wasn't very much call for magic, and nobody ever came to visit Hazel's rickety old cottage. Now, a thick layer of dust covered her magic books, and the cauldron was getting rusty.

"It's not like it used to be!" sighed Hazel, as she sat stroking Mouser one morning. "I can't remember the last time anyone wanted a magic spell. No one even drops in anymore." She sighed again, a long bored sigh. "If I don't get some practice soon, I won't be able to remember any magic at all, and then I really will be a worthless witch. Who ever heard of a witch that can't do magic?"

Hazel decided that it was time to take some action.

"There's only one thing to do!" she announced to the spiders and rats in the cottage. "I'm going to move. Someone, somewhere needs my magic, and I'm going to find them!"

The very next morning, the neighbors in Sunny Drive, Smalltown, watched in amazement as a dark figure on a broomstick flew toward number twenty-four.

As the broomstick nosedived,
Hazel fell to the ground, stood up, dusted off
her magic wand, and, with barely a pause, muttered a quick spell.
"Tongue of newt and tail of mouse, all my stuff come to this house!"

Very slowly, a rusty cauldron, some pots full of slimy gunk, and a huge pile of magic books began to appear in front of Hazel's new home.

"I knew I hadn't lost my touch!" said Hazel, smiling proudly at her own cleverness. But she had spoken too soon.

All of a sudden, the cauldron clattered noisily to the ground and the books spun around in the air, sweeping off Hazel's hat. Then the pots turned upside down, tipping a horrible slimy mess all over the doorstep.

"Fiddlesticks!" cried Hazel, blushing furiously. "I forgot to say the second line of the spell. Silly me! I'd better just clear up this little mess. Lizard's tail and forget-me-nots, back you go into your pots…" Hazel waved her wand in the air wildly, lost her balance, and slipped in the pool of green slime.

By now there was a large crowd of very worried-looking people gathering to watch.

"We've never had a W…W…WITCH as a neighbor before," whispered one very nervous man.

"You never know, it might be useful!" suggested his wife.

"Not if all her magic spells go wrong like that!" said their son, just loud enough for Hazel to hear.

"She looks like a worthless

witch to me!"

65

"What a bad start," sighed Hazel, wiping some sticky green gunge off her cloak and heading inside. "Maybe I should just face the fact that I'm no good at magic anymore."

Mouser arched his back and rubbed against his mistress's legs. He purred comfortingly, until she reached down and scooped him into her arms.

"You're right, Mouser," she said, stroking his head thoughtfully. "It wasn't the best start, but I shouldn't be put off so easily. All I need is a bit of practice. Then they'll see just how helpful I can be!"

The next morning, bright and early, Hazel blew the dust off her magic books and began to thumb through the pages.

"What I need are some useful spells," she decided, flicking through a huge volume entitled *One Thousand Helpful Charms for Everyday Use.*

"Cheeses, sneezes, wheezes..." she muttered, searching for just the right spell.

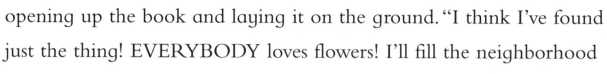

"Frogs, bogs, logs. No, no! Those just won't do! Showers, bowers… Aha!" she cried triumphantly, opening up the book and laying it on the ground. "I think I've found just the thing! EVERYBODY loves flowers! I'll fill the neighborhood with flowers. They'll all be delighted!"

Hazel read the spell carefully, memorizing each line. She was determined not to make a mistake this time. When she was very certain that she had learned every word by heart, she took out her wand and began to chant the spell.

"Wing of bats and fur of possums, fill the gardens up with BLOSSOMS!"

Then she twirled her wand in the air. A golden spark shot out from the end and leaped into a bush. Immediately, the bush burst into flower.

"Wow! This is fun!" cried Hazel, pointing and twirling her wand all around the garden. "I knew all I needed was a bit of practice!"

Golden sparks flew from the end of the wand and flashed into every corner. Wherever the sparks fell, flowers sprang up from the ground, carpeting the gardens in a blanket of blossoms. The neighbors in Sunny Drive could not believe their eyes. They rushed out into the street, and stared in wonder as the happy witch whirled her magic wand, filling the street with flowers of every shape and size.

"I think that's enough now!" said Hazel, when all the gardens were ablaze with color. "Magic, STOP!" she cried. But the magic didn't stop. Her wand just kept flashing golden sparks, and the flowers just kept appearing—more and more and more.

"I'm SURE I said the spell correctly," cried Hazel, panicking. She flicked through the spell book until she found the right page again. "Oh, no!" she wailed. "I didn't notice that the last page of the spell has been torn out! No wonder my magic went wrong!"

Hazel knew there was only one way to stop the spell.
She quickly grabbed her wand and snapped it in two.
Immediately, the magic sparks stopped flying,
but not before the damage was done. The street
was buried under a sea of blossoms, and the crowd of neighbors
(or at least those she could still see) were not looking very friendly.

"Just look what you've done!" yelled the man from next door,
shaking his fist. "It will take days to clean up this mess."

"Don't worry!" replied Hazel cheerfully. "I can fix this in a jiffy. I'll
go and get my spare wand."

"Oh, no, you don't!" cried the woman from
across the street furiously. "We don't
need any more of your tricks or
magic spells. You're a worthless
witch."

"Please don't be angry," begged
Hazel. "I didn't mean to make a
mess. I was only trying to be
helpful. If you give me a
chance, I know I can
make it up to you all."

The crowd looked at Hazel suspiciously. "How do we know we can trust you?" asked one woman, speaking for everyone.

"All I want to do is help," said Hazel. "Please let me try just one more time. Just tell me what you want me to do."

"Well, all right," replied the woman,, in a slightly friendlier voice. "But this is your last chance. Do you see that dark cloud over there?" She pointed to a big black cloud in the sky above the school athletic field. "Well, it's the school spring fair today," she continued, "and we don't want it to rain. Can you make the cloud disappear?"

Hazel was delighted. Making the sun come out used to be her favorite spell.

"I KNOW I can do it," she beamed happily.

Hazel got her spare wand, polished it up, and began to say the magic spell. The crowd looked on with interest.

"Spider's leg and bag of fleas, vanish raincloud on the bree… …ahh…ahh… ahhh…CHOO!" There were so many blossoms in the street that it made Hazel sneeze loudly, right in the middle of the spell.

"Oops! I blew it!" said Hazel in alarm. Everyone gazed up at the sky nervously. Instead of disappearing, huge drops of rain began to fall from the big black cloud. And it didn't just rain. It poured, right over the school.

"Fiddle! Faddle! Fuddle!" cried Hazel, looking at the disappointed faces in the crowd. "Now I've ruined the school fair, too.

I really am a worthless witch. I may as well go back to my rickety old cottage right now."

Hazel felt so guilty about what she had done that she began to pack to leave that very evening. Even Mouser couldn't cheer her up. "It's time I retired," she told the little cat sadly. "No one around here will ever want my help now."

Suddenly, there was a loud knock at the door.

"I'm sorry about ruining the school fair," began Hazel as she opened the door, expecting to see an angry crowd.

"Sorry?" replied the man on the doorstep, smiling in surprise. "There's no need to be sorry. I am the school principal, and I've come to thank you. There was a fire at the school this afternoon.

Your rainstorm put out the flames and saved our school. You are a local heroine!"

Hazel could hardly believe her ears. "You mean I really am a helpful witch?" she asked in amazement.

"You certainly are," nodded the principal. "And I'm not the only one who thinks so," he added, leading her out into the front yard. There in the street were all her neighbors, clapping and cheering as loudly as they could.

"Three cheers for Hazel!" they roared. "The best and most helpful witch in Smalltown!"

"Thank you," beamed Hazel, flushing with pride, and waving at the crowds. "I knew I could do it," she whispered to Mouser, who was busy rubbing against her legs. "Although, between you and me, Mouser, I still think I may need a little more practice!"

Snow White

Once there were a king and queen who lived in a distant land. They were very happy, except for one thing—they had no children.

"Oh," said the queen, "how I wish I had a daughter with skin as white as snow, hair as black as a raven's wing, and lips as red as cherries."

Within a year the queen's wish was granted and they had a beautiful baby girl, whom they called Snow White. Soon after her birth, the poor queen died and the king eventually remarried.

The new queen was very beautiful, but also very vain and very wicked. She could not bear to think that anyone was more beautiful than she was. Every day she would stand in front of a magic mirror, and say:

"Mirror, mirror, on the wall, Who is the fairest of them all?" And the mirror would reply: *"You are the fairest one of all."*

However, as the years passed, Snow White grew up to become more and more beautiful, until one day the magic mirror told the wicked queen: *"You were the fairest, shining bright, But now much fairer is Snow White."* The queen was furious. She sent for a servant. She told the servant to take Snow White into the forest and leave her there for the wild animals to eat.

And so it was that Snow White found herself alone in the forest. At first she was scared, but soon the animals took pity on her and led her to a pretty little cottage. She knocked on the door and, when there was no answer, she walked right in. The inside of the cottage was as pretty as the outside. In the middle of the room stood a neat little table, set with seven places and surrounded by seven little chairs.

Feeling hungry and thirsty, Snow White took a little bread from each of the plates and a little milk from each of the cups. Then, feeling tired, she curled up on one of the seven beds and fell into a deep sleep.

The cottage belonged to seven dwarfs. Every morning they left their cottage to dig for jewels and gold in the hills.

And every evening they returned home to eat and sleep.

When they returned home that night, they noticed at once that they had a visitor.

"Somebody has been eating my bread," said one.

"Somebody has been drinking my milk," said another.

"Somebody has been sleeping in my bed," said another. "Look, she's still here!"

Quickly, all the dwarfs gathered around the bed to look at their sleeping visitor.

"Isn't she lovely?" said one.

"Let's leave her to sleep," said another. And so they left her until morning.

When Snow White awoke, the seven little dwarfs were gathered around her bed. They were so kind that she told them her story.

The dwarfs all agreed that Snow White should stay with them. Each day, when they went to dig for jewels and gold in the hills, Snow White stayed home, cleaning and cooking.

And so the years passed, and Snow White grew more and more beautiful.

Meanwhile the queen, thinking that Snow White was dead, hadn't bothered looking in her mirror. Then one day, she thought she felt a pimple growing on her chin and went to the mirror to check. While she was there, she asked:

"Mirror, mirror, on the wall,

Who is the fairest of them all?"

You can just imagine her surprise when it replied:

"In the dwarfs' house, in yonder hill, Snow White is the fairest still."

The queen turned red with fury. Determined to get rid of Snow White once and for all, she quickly began to plot and plan.

The next morning the queen dressed up as an old woman. Then she filled a basket with pretty things and went to the dwarfs' cottage.

"Buy something from a poor old woman," she cackled. Of course, Snow White, being such a kind-hearted young girl, let her in at once.

"Oh, these are ever so pretty," said Snow White, pulling some ribbons from the basket.

"Yes, just perfect for lacing your dress," agreed the old woman. Snow White let the old woman lace her dress with a colorful ribbon.

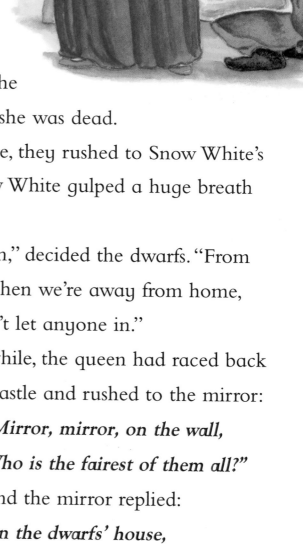

But the wicked queen pulled the ribbon so tight that Snow White fell to the ground. The wicked queen thought that she was dead.

When the seven dwarfs arrived home, they rushed to Snow White's side and quickly untied the ribbon. Snow White gulped a huge breath and soon recovered.

"It must have been the wicked queen," decided the dwarfs. "From now on you must always be watchful. When we're away from home, you mustn't let anyone in."

Meanwhile, the queen had raced back to the castle and rushed to the mirror:

"Mirror, mirror, on the wall,

Who is the fairest of them all?"

And the mirror replied:

"In the dwarfs' house,

in yonder hill,

Snow White is the fairest still."

79

The queen couldn't believe her ears. Once again, she began to plot and plan.

In the morning, the queen called at the dwarfs' house, dressed as a beggar woman with a basket of pretty combs— combs she had dipped in poison!

"I can't let you in," Snow White shouted from the window.

"Never mind," croaked the old woman.

"Why don't you just try this pretty comb in your lovely hair?"

The comb was so pretty that Snow White leaned out of the window and allowed the old woman to push it into her hair. As soon as the comb touched Snow White's skin, she fell to the ground.

Luckily for Snow White, the seven dwarfs came home early that day. When they saw her lying there, they guessed what had happened and removed the comb from her hair at once. Again, Snow White was quick to recover. Once again, the dwarfs warned her about strangers.

The queen, meanwhile, was in a rage, for she had just been told:

> *"In the dwarfs' house, in yonder hill,*
> *Snow White is the fairest still."*

Now she was more determined than ever to destroy Snow White. So the next morning, she picked an apple that was half red and half green, and injected poison into one half of it. Then, dressed as a farmer's wife, she called on Snow White.

"I just want to give you this juicy apple," smiled the farmer's wife, holding up the half-red and half-green apple. "Look, it's not poisoned. I'll take a bite from it myself." And she took a bite from the half of the apple that wasn't poisoned.

Seeing that the apple did the farmer's wife no harm, Snow White accepted it and took a bite. But as soon as she did, she fell down as if dead.

That night, when the dwarfs got home, there was nothing they could do to wake Snow White, for, although she was not dead, she was in a very deep sleep—a sleep so deep that it seemed as though she would never wake.

Feeling very sad, the seven dwarfs built her a glass coffin and placed her in the hills, where all who passed could admire her beauty, for, although she slept for year after year, her beauty never changed. Her skin remained as white as snow, her hair was as black as a raven's wing, and her lips were as red as cherries.

Then one day, a handsome prince saw the glass coffin and fell in love with the sleeping princess.

"You must let me take her back to my castle," said the prince. "I cannot live without seeing such beauty each day."

At first the dwarfs were reluctant to agree, but finally they saw that the prince loved Snow White, and they agreed to let him take her.

Very carefully, the seven dwarves lifted the glass coffin onto their shoulders and started down the hillside. But they stumbled, and the piece of poisoned apple was shaken from Snow White's throat.

She awoke at once. And, on seeing the prince, she too fell in love.

It was a grand wedding. The whole kingdom was invited, and all agreed that the bride was the fairest of them all.

Meanwhile, the wicked queen had discovered that her evil plan had failed. In her anger, she smashed her mirror and never looked at her reflection again.

Anya and the Magic Carpet

Far away, in a distant land, there was a sultan's grand palace, where many people lived. Among them was a small servant girl called Anya. Anya was a lovely girl, who worked very hard.

One day, Anya was clearing the table when she heard Cook calling her from the kitchen. As usual, she sounded very angry.

"Here I am, Cook," called Anya. "I was clearing the table…"

"Well, hurry up, then!" snapped Cook, snatching the tray from Anya. But as she grabbed it, the plates slid off and clattered to the floor.

"Now look what you've made me do!" Cook shouted. "Just get out from under my feet before you do any more harm!"

Anya ran from the room, and disappeared up a flight of dusty stairs that led to an attic in the palace tower.

This was Anya's secret hiding place. No one bothered her here—not even the rats that gnawed at the carpets stored there.

Anya unrolled one of the carpets and sat down. Then, as she had done a thousand times before, she took the broken locket from around her neck and gazed at the woman in the picture inside. The smiling face always made her feel better.

This battered old locket was the only thing that Anya owned! For as long as she could remember, she had worked as a maid in the palace. Everyone told her she should be happy. "You could be out on the street like the other orphans," they said. But Anya didn't feel happy. She felt lonely and unloved.

"I wish I had someone to love me," she sighed, as a teardrop rolled down her cheek and landed with a plop on the floor.

Suddenly, the carpet beneath her gave a sharp jerk. Then it slid along the dusty attic floor, took off and floated in midair!

"A MAGIC carpet!" exclaimed Anya in amazement. "I thought they only existed in fairy tales!"

The carpet shivered as if to disagree, then began to fly madly around the room, zooming between the rafters.

"Whoa! Where are you taking me?" laughed Anya, as the magic carpet headed straight out the open window, into the cool night air. It felt wonderful! Faster and faster the carpet flew, high above the city rooftops. Then, when the city was far behind them, it swooped down and hovered above a beautiful pool, where animals were taking a nighttime drink. As the magic carpet moved slowly among the animals, Anya reached out to greet each one in turn.

The carpet landed beside a friendly deer, and Anya hopped down and took a long drink from the pond. The water tasted delicious. Anya smiled happily.

Then Anya climbed back on the carpet and they were off once more. Anya clung tightly as they flew over mountains and seas. She'd never realized that the world outside the palace was quite so big.

Before long, they were in a town where Anya had never been before. The carpet swooped down and flew past the windows of grand houses. How Anya laughed to see the surprise on people's faces as they flew past.

Finally, the carpet landed with a thud on the riverbank. "Phew!" gasped Anya. "That was a bumpy landing!"

"Who are you?" asked a voice.

Anya turned to see an old lady sitting on a bench by the river. The lady's face was kind, but Anya had never seen such sad-looking eyes.

"I'm Anya," she said shyly. "I'm sorry I landed in your garden…"

But the old lady didn't seem to hear. She was too busy gazing up at the stars. Anya watched her face in silence. It was strange, but she felt they had met before—but that was impossible, wasn't it?

"I love stars, don't you?" said Anya, hoping to make the lady speak again. "Sometimes I wish on them!"

The woman smiled sadly. "I wish on them, too!" she sighed. "I wish that one day I will find my granddaughter!" A tear rolled down her cheek as she continued. "She was lost in a storm at sea. Her parents are dead now, but I have spent seven years searching for her."

"How terrible!" said Anya.

Just then, a moonbeam shone on the broken locket around Anya's neck. The old lady jumped to her feet and grasped the necklace in her hands. "Where did you get this?" she asked excitedly.

"I don't know," answered Anya. "I'm an orphan. I was found with it around my neck as a baby."

Trembling, the old lady reached inside her cloak and pulled out a broken locket, exactly like Anya's. With shaking hands, she pressed the two halves together. They fitted perfectly!

"What does it all mean?" gasped Anya.

"It means that you are my granddaughter!" cried the old lady joyfully. "My daughter broke this locket in two when you were born.

She gave half to each of us. That is her picture inside."

"So now I really do have somebody to love me!" whispered Anya in disbelief.

"You do!" replied the old lady, hugging Anya. "And now that I have found you, I will never let you go again!"

Just then, Anya felt a nudge behind her. It was the magic carpet. "You brought me here on purpose, didn't you!" cried Anya happily.

"Thank you for making my wish come true!"

But the carpet just swayed gently before them, then swooped up through the trees, and disappeared from sight.

"I wonder where it will go next?" smiled Anya, taking her grandmother's arm. "Off to make someone else's wish come true, I hope!"

89

Cinderella

Long ago, in a distant land, there lived a man with his beautiful daughter. They were both very happy, until one day the man took a new wife. The new wife was not a kind woman and, to make matters worse, she had two bad-tempered daughters. The two daughters were so mean and so ugly that they were jealous of the man's beautiful daughter. Indeed, they were so jealous that they took away all her fine clothes and forced her to work as their maid.

The poor girl worked from dawn to dusk. She cooked all the meals, cleaned all the rooms, and looked after all the fires. And when she wasn't working around the house, the ugly sisters insisted that she dress them and brush their hair.

At night, while the ugly sisters snored in their fine beds, their beautiful stepsister huddled among the cinders beside the fire. This was why she always looked so dusty and sooty that everyone called her Cinderella.

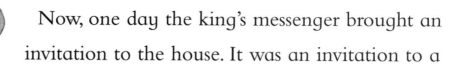

Now, one day the king's messenger brought an invitation to the house. It was an invitation to a ball that the king was giving for his son, the prince. All the young girls in the land were invited, so that the prince could choose a bride.

The ugly sisters were delighted, and immediately started discussing what they were going to wear.

"Can I come, too?" asked Cinderella. "I've never been to a ball."

"Of course you can't, silly," laughed Cinderella's stepmother, pointing to the rags she wore. "What would you wear? Besides, no prince would bother looking at a silly, sooty face like yours. But don't worry, you can help my girls get dressed for the ball."

On the evening of the ball, the ugly sisters took ages getting ready. Poor Cinderella's head whirled as they barked orders at her.

"Tighter, tighter!" cried one, as Cinderella struggled to fasten a corset around her huge waist.

"Ouch! That hurt!" snapped the other, as Cinderella tried to tease the knots from her tangled hair.

When at last they left for the ball, Cinderella fell to the floor and wept. "If only I could go to the ball," she sobbed.

"But you shall," said a kind voice. Cinderella wiped the tears from her eyes and looked up to see her fairy godmother standing before her.

As you can imagine, Cinderella was very surprised. She hadn't even known that she had a fairy godmother until that moment. "But I don't have a thing to wear," she said. "And I don't have a coach, so I'd never get there in time."

"Just fetch these things," said the fairy godmother, pulling out a list from up her sleeve, "and I'll get you there before you know it."

Cinderella looked at the list and frowned. But, being a good girl, she quickly did as she was asked. Five minutes later, she returned with the things on the list: a pumpkin, six white mice, a frog, and two lizards.

Her fairy godmother drew out her magic wand and touched the pumpkin. Immediately it turned into a golden coach.

Then she touched the mice with her wand, and they turned into six white horses. Next she touched the frog, which turned into a smart coachman. And finally, she touched the two lizards, who turned into two well-dressed footmen.

"And now for you," said the fairy godmother, pointing her wand at Cinderella. Instantly, Cinderella's rags were transformed into a fine velvet ball gown, and the clogs she usually wore on her feet were turned into delicate glass slippers.

"Now, go to your ball and enjoy yourself," said the fairy godmother. "But remember this. You must leave the ball before midnight, for on the stroke of twelve the magic will run out and all will be as it was before."

The footmen helped Cinderella into the coach, the coachman took up the reins, and they were on their way.

When Cinderella arrived at the ball, everyone gasped at her beauty. "May I have this dance?" asked the prince. And, of course, Cinderella agreed.

For the rest of the evening, the prince would dance with no other. Cinderella's ugly sisters didn't recognize her, dressed as she was in such fine clothes. But they were still furious.

"I can't imagine what the prince sees in her. She's nothing but a skinny beanpole," sneered one.

"Barely a jewel in sight," sneered the other.

It was the best evening of Cinderella's life.

She enjoyed herself so much that she almost forgot about her fairy godmother's warning. Then, just before twelve, she remembered.

"I must leave," she told the prince. Before he could stop her, she had fled into the night. But as she raced out of the palace, she slipped on the steps and lost one of her glass slippers. She dared not stop. She didn't even notice that the prince picked up the slipper.

Then, as the clock struck twelve, Cinderella's ball gown vanished and she found herself in her rags once more. When she got to where she had left the coach, she found the pumpkin in its place.

Poor Cinderella had to run all the way home. She only just made it before her stepmother and stepsisters returned.

The next day, the prince announced that he would travel the kingdom in search of the owner of the dainty slipper. "Every girl in the kingdom will try it for size," he declared, "for whoever it fits is the one I love, and the one I will make my bride."

Of course, every girl in the kingdom was eager to marry the prince. Girls of all shapes and sizes tried to squeeze their foot into the tiny slipper, but it was too small.

At last the prince arrived at Cinderella's house. Cinderella's stepmother was determined that one of her daughters would become the prince's bride.

"Push harder," she hissed, trying to wedge the glass slipper onto one of her daughters' feet.

"Can't you do anything right?" she complained, when her other daughter couldn't even get the slipper over her lumpy toes.

"Don't you have another daughter?" asked the prince, when Cinderella's stepmother finally admitted defeat.

"There is only Cinderella," she said, "and she's little more than a maid."

But the prince insisted that Cinderella try on the slipper and, of course, it fitted her perfectly. The prince peered at the shabby figure before him and smiled. Even through the dirt and grime, he could recognize the beautiful maiden he had danced with.

"My one true love," he cried, before lifting her onto his horse and riding away.

Puppy Love

Buster yawned, pushed past his brothers and sisters, and fell out of the basket. He trotted over to his bowl, helped himself to some water, and waited for the other puppies to wake up. Right now, they were still fast asleep. Four golden-haired little puppies that looked exactly like Ellie, their beautiful mother.

Ellie had given birth to nine puppies altogether. Sometimes they all wriggled together into a big sleepy pile; other times they chased around, nipping each other's ears and pretending to be big, fierce grown-up dogs. The other puppies loved to tease Buster, calling him "Patch," but Buster didn't care, he loved being part of the golden-haired puppy gang.

After a few weeks,

strangers began to visit the house in search of their dream puppy. All of them said how beautiful the puppies were, and nobody left the house without choosing at least one of them.

Soon there were only five puppies left.

"I suppose," Bertie the cat remarked to Buster, "that you are expecting somebody to take you away any day now?"

Buster stopped playing with his smallest sister and blinked. He hadn't really thought about leaving home.

"Well, yes," he said at last. "I suppose so. Though I'll be sad to leave Mom and the others, of course."

"I wouldn't worry too much about that," smirked the cat. "I very much doubt that anyone will choose you."

"Why?" asked Buster.

"Take a look in the mirror," smiled Bertie. "That should give you a clue."

Buster trotted over and looked in the mirror. Staring out at him was a little brown-and-white dog with a patch over one round brown eye.

"Who's that?" asked Buster, puzzled.

"That's you, silly!" snorted Bertie.

"Me? But I look nothing like Mom and my brothers and sisters," he said in a small voice.

"Exactly," said Bertie.

"You're just special," said his mother, when Buster told her what Bertie had said. "Don't listen to Bertie."

But Buster knew that Bertie was right. Nobody would choose him.

That afternoon, a boy and a girl chose Buster's smallest sister.

"I suppose it's because I'm so pretty!" she said, waving goodbye to Buster.

"She's right!" hissed Bertie. "A funny-looking thing like you will never find a home."

Soon there were just two puppies left.

"Time's running out," said Bertie. "At this rate, you'll be going to the pound. You can't stay here forever, you know."

When the doorbell rang the next morning, Buster barely bothered looking up from his basket.

"Pick me," barked Buster's brother. "See how cute and golden I am, not funny-looking like old 'Patch' here."

Buster sighed. He knew that his brother was right; nobody would want a puppy that looked like him. But, to Buster's surprise, when the door opened, two golden-haired girls went straight for him. One lifted him into the air.

"Look, Mommy!" she cried. "He's just like the puppy in Lucy's book. And look at his collar. He's even called Buster! We've got to choose him."

"He's perfect," smiled their mother. "Lucy will love him."

"Oh, no, she won't," thought Buster.

But Buster soon found himself driving away with his new family.

At last, the car stopped in front of a small red-brick house. Buster was picked up and taken inside. There was a lot of whispering and giggling, which Buster didn't understand at all. Then he found himself being bundled into a small back room. "Oh, dear," thought Buster. "Is this the pound? Is this where I get left all by myself? He laid his head on his paws and waited.

Before long, the girls' father came into the room. "Come on, boy," he said kindly, picking Buster up. He tied a red ribbon around Buster's neck, and carried him to a bright, sunny room. The mother and the two blonde girls were kneeling on the floor among a small pile of presents. Sitting between them was a smiling little girl that Buster hadn't seen before. She was younger than the others, with an untidy mop of red hair, a freckly face, and a pair of round brown eyes. A little girl who looked nothing like her golden-haired mother or sisters!

"Happy birthday, Lucy," beamed the two blonde girls.

At the sight of Buster, Lucy sat down on the floor and smiled. Buster threw himself into her arms, and Lucy hugged him tight.

"Well," laughed her mother, "what do you think of him?"

Buster held his breath. Was she going to say he was ugly? Was she going to want to send him back to his old house?

"He's perfect," Lucy breathed. "He's exactly the kind of puppy I've always wanted. I'm going to call him Buster, like the one in my book!"

The Snow Queen

Once there was a wicked magician who enjoyed making mischief. The worst, thing he ever did was make a magical mirror. This mirror was like no other, for it made everything reflected in it appear ugly. Beautiful fields looked like marshy swamps, and the prettiest people looked like old hags.

The magician was so proud of his mirror that he flew around the world with it, causing trouble. One day, when he was flying above the earth, he laughed so much over the misery his mirror caused that the mirror slipped from his hands and fell to the earth to splinter into a million pieces.

The splinters flew all over the place. Some stuck in people's hearts and made them cold and hard. Other tiny specks blew into people's eyes and made everything they saw appear twisted and ugly.

The largest piece of all fell on the Snow Queen, who ruled the icy lands of the north. From that moment on, she became the coldest and meanest woman who ever lived.

Meanwhile, far away from the Snow Queen's chilly home, lived a little boy and a little girl, called Kay and Gerda. Kay and Gerda were the best of friends and loved each other dearly. Every day they played together, even in the winter when the Snow Queen blew her icy breath across the land.

One winter's day, Kay and Gerda were making a snowman in the village square when Kay let out a cry.

"Ah! Something flew in my eye," he cried. "And I felt a pain in my heart." Alas, splinters from the magical mirror had fallen on Kay.

"Can I do anything?" asked Gerda.

"Get lost!" shouted Kay, before kicking over the snowman. When Gerda started to cry, Kay laughed. Then he grabbed his little sled and sped away.

Kay played alone in the snow until a big sleigh stopped nearby. Kay could not see who was driving the sleigh but he did not care. He tied his sled to the back of the sleigh, so when it pulled away it took him with it.

On and on went the sleigh, dragging Kay behind it, until it reached an icy palace. Once there, the driver of the sleigh got down and called to Kay in an icy voice.

"Come here, Kay, you must be freezing." It was the Snow Queen.

Kay wasn't at all afraid. He wasn't even scared when the Snow Queen bent down and gave him an icy kiss on the cheek. The kiss cast a spell over Kay. It made him forget all about Gerda and think that the Snow Queen was the most perfect person he'd ever seen. But, worst of all, it froze his heart!

Back home, Gerda had searched high and low for Kay. Everyone in the village had joined in, but Kay was nowhere to be found.

"Perhaps he has fallen in the river," an old man suggested.

Gerda took her best red shoes and threw them into the river, begging the river to give back Kay in return. But the river had not seen Kay, and the red shoes were swept back.

"How will I find him?" wept Gerda. As if in answer, a little boat appeared at the riverbank. Gerda climbed aboard the boat and was swept down the stream. On and on she went, through lands and kingdoms she'd never even known existed.

At last the boat came to a halt in a forest.

"Where am I?" Gerda asked a passing reindeer.

"Lapland," replied the reindeer.

"Have you seen a little boy with blond hair?" asked Gerda.

"I think such a boy is living with the Snow Queen in the north," said the reindeer. "Jump on my back and I'll help you in your search."

The reindeer galloped day and night until they reached the Snow Queen's palace. As Gerda stood outside the icy walls, she shivered with fear. But she knew that it was up to her to rescue Kay.

Inside the palace, Kay was cold and alone. The Snow Queen was away, and all Kay had for entertainment were some chips of ice. The Snow Queen had told him that he could go home if he could make them spell the word "FREE." But, no matter how hard Kay tried, he could not do it.

When Gerda saw her beloved friend, she rushed to his side. She held him in her arms and wept as she realized that he did not even recognize her. Her tears were so pure and full of love that when they fell on Kay's chest, they melted his frozen heart.

Kay began to cry, too. As he cried the splinter of glass was washed from his eye. And when he looked down at the chips of ice, they had arranged themselves into the word "FREE"!

Kay hugged Gerda with joy. "You're the best friend a boy could wish for," he smiled.

Their tears of sorrow were quickly replaced with tears of joy.

"Come on, let's go home," laughed Gerda. And after that Kay and Gerda never argued again.

The Little Dragon
Learns to Fly

Long, long ago, a fierce dragon lived in a mountain cave above a village called Dragonia. Nobody had actually seen the dragon, but many people had seen the hot flames of dragon's breath that poured from the cave when anybody went too close.

One day, a little boy called Jake was picking wildflowers near the cave when he stubbed his toe on what looked like a rock.

"Ouch!" said the rock, which jumped up and hid behind a bigger rock. Jack was stunned.

It wasn't a rock at all.

"I was taking a n…n…n…nap," complained a frightened voice.

"Who are you?" asked Jake.

"I'm the d…d…d…dragon, and if you d…d…d…don't go away I will b…b…b…b…breathe fire all over you," stuttered the voice. After a pause it added, "Are you big?"

"I'm bigger than my brother," said Jake. "I'm seven."

A bumpy green head, with pointy ears and nostrils on stalks, peered around the rock.

"That's funny," said the dragon. "I'm seven too."

He came out from behind the rock. He was a surprisingly small dragon. In fact, he was no taller than Jake, with stumpy wings on his back no bigger than Jake's hands.

"Can you fly?" asked Jake.

"I've never tried," said the dragon.

"Never?" gasped Jake.

"No, never." The very idea of flying made him tremble. "Now, please go away and don't tell anyone I'm only a small dragon, or people will start poking around in my cave and frighten me." Then he disappeared.

By the time Jake reached the village he was bursting to tell someone about the little dragon. But when he remembered how scared he had been, he decided not to. And that would have been that, if the villagers hadn't been so poor that they held a meeting to decide how to get rich.

"I know," suggested the butcher, "let's get a knight to slay the dragon and charge money for people to watch."

That was in the days when people did that sort of thing, and so the villagers all agreed that it was a brilliant idea. They invited the local knight to fight the dragon.

You should have seen the crowd that turned up. They all cheered like mad when the knight set off up the mountain. Jake didn't see him go. He was already scurrying up the mountain to warn the dragon. Because he was in such a hurry, he didn't look where he was going and slipped.

"*Ahhhh!*" he cried, as he hurtled helter-skelter down the side of the mountain! He landed with a bump on a narrow ledge.

"Help! Help!" he called. But nobody heard, except the dragon, who was soon peering down at him.

"Help me," begged Jake.

"What?" asked the dragon, who was quaking with fear. "How can I possibly help?"

"Couldn't you flap your wings and fly to my rescue?" asked Jake.

"Don't be silly! I've never flown in my life," replied the dragon.

"But," pleaded Jake, "I was climbing up the mountain to warn you that a knight is coming to kill you."

"Ooooooh," said the dragon. "I'm gone!"

Poor Jake. He was so frightened he couldn't help crying. The dragon, who hadn't gone very far, knew all about crying. It was very lonely being a dragon and living by yourself. So he cried a lot.

"Please don't cry," he said, peering down at Jake again.

"But I might die."

"Oh, dear. Couldn't you climb back up?"

"No!" sobbed Jake.

"I'll bet you haven't even tried!" said the dragon angrily. He stamped his foot so hard that the ground beneath him began to crumble, and he began to fall.

"WHOOOOAH!" he cried, as he hurtled down the side of the mountain.

"Oooooooh!" he yelled, whizzing past the narrow ledge where Jake sat.

"Flap your wings and fly!" yelled Jake.

"Oooooooh," sobbed the dragon.

"Fly!" begged Jake.

Goodness knows what made the dragon twitch his wings. But something did. The next moment, he was flying!

"Look, look, I can fly!" he gasped, scooping Jake from the ledge and flap-flapping to the top of the mountain.

"How about that?" he laughed, dropping Jake, not very gently, at the mouth of his cave.

"Ah, there you are!" panted a voice. It was the knight. He was out of breath from hurrying up the mountain in his heavy suit of armor.

"Please don't kill the dragon," begged Jake.

"Y…yes, please don't kill me," quaked the dragon.

"I wouldn't dream of it," exclaimed the knight. "Why, I saw this brave dragon throw himself off the mountain just so he could fly to your rescue. It was one of the bravest things I've ever seen."

Which is what the knight told the villagers when he brought Jake down the mountain.

The villagers were so pleased that they threw a special feast in honor of the little dragon. There was dancing and singing, sandwiches and cakes, and lots and lots to drink. Everyone had a splendid time, including the little dragon, who Jake managed to persuade to join them.

The little dragon made so many new friends that he couldn't remember all their names. He'd never been so happy. Indeed, he was so happy that he decided to share his treasure with all the villagers, for, as I'm sure you know, all dragons guard a hoard of treasure.

And so the villagers were no longer poor, and the dragon was no longer lonely, and everybody lived happily ever after!

The Elves
and the Shoemaker

There was once a shoemaker who lived with his wife. The shoemaker worked very hard, but he never made much money. In time, he became poorer and poorer. Then one day all he had left was one piece of leather. Just enough leather to make one pair of shoes. So that night, before going to bed, the shoemaker cut out the leather and left it on his workbench, ready to sew in the morning.

That night the shoemaker had a restless night's sleep as he worried about what they would do once the leather was gone. But when the shoemaker went to the bench in the morning, he couldn't believe his eyes. In place of the cut-out pieces of leather, there stood the finest pair of shoes he'd ever seen. Every stitch on them was so small and neat that they could hardly be seen.

"I've never seen such shoes," the shoemaker told his wife. They couldn't imagine who might have sewn them. But they proudly displayed them in the window anyway.

Later that morning, a grand lady came into the shop and tried them on. "I've never worn anything so comfortable," she declared. And she paid the shoemaker twice his normal price for them.

The shoemaker was delighted. Now he had money to buy food and enough leather to make two pairs of shoes.

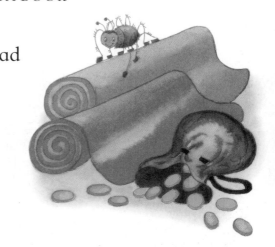

That evening, he carefully cut out the two pairs of shoes. Then he left them on his workbench, ready to stitch in the morning.

The next morning, the shoemaker was delighted to see two pairs of shoes in place of the leather. Once again, they were beautifully stitched.

Later that day, a noble lord came into the shop to buy shoes. The shoemaker showed him the two pairs, and he was so impressed that he tried both on. They fitted perfectly, so he bought both pairs for a lot of money.

Now the shoemaker had enough money to buy leather for four pairs of shoes.

That evening, before going to bed, he carefully cut out the four pairs of shoes and left them on the bench. Once again, he fully intended to stitch them in the morning.

However, when he awoke the next morning, he found four perfect pairs of shoes sitting on his workbench. Once again, he sold the shoes for a great deal of money.

And so it went on. Each night the shoemaker cut out shoes ready to stitch in the morning. And each morning, he found in their place shoes so perfectly made that he couldn't see a bad stitch on them.

Day after day, rich customers came to the shoemaker's shop to buy the perfectly made shoes. So, in time, the shoemaker and his wife became quite rich. But they never took their good fortune for granted.

One evening, just before Christmas, the shoemaker said to his wife, "Why don't we stay up this evening to see who stitches our shoes?"

The shoemaker's wife quickly agreed, and that night they hid behind some clothes hanging in the corner of the room, and waited.

For a long time nothing happened. Then at midnight two tiny little men danced into the room. The two little men, whom the shoemaker recognized as elves, had bare feet and were dressed in rags.

The two elves did not see the shoemaker and his wife, but climbed up onto the bench, sat down, and began stitching. They worked so fast that the shoemaker could hardly believe his eyes. They did not stop until all the work was done. Then they danced off into the night.

The next morning the shoemaker and his wife agreed that they should repay the elves in some way. After all, they had made them rich.

So that very day, they went out and bought the finest material and the softest leather they could find. And that evening, they got to work making new clothes for the elves.

Night after night they worked on the clothes. At last, on Christmas Eve, everything was ready. Instead of leaving shoes on the bench, the shoemaker and his wife laid out the perfectly made outfits. Then they hid and waited.

At midnight, the elves danced into the room and climbed up onto the bench. They were surprised to see tiny matching outfits instead of shoes for stitching. Delighted, they dressed themselves in their new clothes. Then, laughing and singing, they danced out into the night.

After that, the shoemaker and his wife never saw the elves again. But they did not mind. They had repaid the favor, and from then on luck was always with them. In time they became very rich, and lived a long and happy life together.

The Trouble with Finley

Finley was the friendliest gnome in the forest. He was never angry, and he always had time to smile and joke with his friends. "Good luck," he'd cry whenever he saw George the gnome with his fishing rod. "Let me help," he'd say to Trixie Pixie whenever he saw her sprinkling morning dew.

So you can imagine everyone's surprise when, one morning, Finley was in a very bad mood.

"Good morning, Finley!" said Trixie Pixie.

"GOOD?" frowned Finley. "What's good about it?" Then he turned his back on Trixie Pixie. Trixie Pixie stared at Finley in amazement. What was wrong with him?

He was usually so polite and friendly.

Just then, George the gnome puffed past on his way to the river. "Heard any good jokes lately, Finley?" he waved.

"You trying to fish—that's a joke," replied Finley rudely. And with that, he marched inside, slamming the door behind him.

"That's not like Finley!" gasped George. "I think we ought to find out what the problem is right away."

Later that morning, Trixie Pixie and George called a meeting to see if anyone knew what was making Finley so grumpy.

The air was filled with excited chattering as pixies, gnomes, fairies, and goblins tried to guess what was wrong.

"Perhaps Finley has a toothache," suggested Gobble. "That always makes me grumpy."

"Finley has false teeth," replied George, "so it can't be that."

"Maybe he's hungry?" suggested Rosey Fairy. "I get angry when I'm hungry."

"Finley always has a big breakfast," said Trixie Pixie. "It must be something else."

Suddenly a voice piped up from the back of the crowd. "I know what's wrong!" said Pebble, who was one of the smartest pixies in the forest. "He's not getting enough sleep. I heard him complain that the noise of the stream next to his house is keeping him awake at night. THAT'S why he's so grumpy."

"Pebble's right!" cried George, jumping up and down with excitement. "I've heard Finley complain about the stream, too. But how can we fix that? We can't stop the stream from bubbling."

"I know what to do to help Finley get to sleep!" said Pebble. "All we need is a little bit of help from the animals in the forest! Now gather round and I'll tell you my plan."

"I do hope that stream doesn't keep me awake again," said Finley to himself as he was getting ready for bed that night. "I really do need a good night's sleep for a change."

He was just about to jump into bed when suddenly he heard a loud noise outside his bedroom window.

126

TAP! TAP! TAP!

The noise got louder and louder and quicker and quicker.

TAP! TAP! TAP! TAP! TAP!

"What on earth…!" cried Finley, poking a very grumpy face out of the window. There, on a branch above his window perched a woodpecker, busily pecking a hole in the trunk. "Can't a fellow get any peace around here?" growled Finley, slamming the window shut and stuffing his hanky in his ears.

Finley folded back his bedclothes, filled his hot-water bottle, and climbed into bed. But just as he was snuggling down under the covers he heard a buzzing noise. Bzzzzz!

The noise got louder and louder, and closer and closer.

BZZZZZZZZZZZ!

Finley leaped out of bed and threw open the window again. There, hanging from the windowsill, was a hive of bees, buzzing noisily.

"Really!" moaned Finley. "What a time of night to be making such a racket."

Finley turned off the light and snuggled down again. SCRAPE! Finley sat bolt upright in bed.

SCRAPE! SCRAPE! SCRAPE!

"NOW WHAT?" he shouted, marching across the room. He threw open the window and looked down. There, among the roots of the tree was a rabbit, digging a burrow.

"PLEASE let me get to sleep!" cried Finley, as he climbed back into bed and pulled his pillow over his head. But he could still hear TAP! TAP! TAP! BZZZ! BZZZ! BZZZ! SCRAPE! SCRAPE!

Just when Finley thought he would go mad, the noise suddenly stopped. All he could hear was the sound of the bubbling stream that flowed beside his home. After all the loud noises, it was like a gentle lullaby, singing the exhausted gnome to sleep.

Finley sighed a huge happy sigh. "At last!" he smiled, snuggling down under the covers.

Before long, all that could be heard in the little house was the sound of the happy gnome's snores.

The next morning, it was a very different Finley who met his friends at the garden gate. "Good morning!" he cried, as George walked past with his fishing rod. "Thank you," he chuckled, as Trixie Pixie skipped past, sprinkling dew. Finley was himself again!

"You seem happy today," said Pebble as he strolled past Finley's gate.

"I am!" agreed Finley, smiling at the clever pixie. "It's amazing what a good night's sleep can do for you. I slept wonderfully well last night. You know, I think the noise of the stream is really lovely!"

Pebble winked knowingly at the others. "I guess anything is better than all the noise our helpers made," he grinned.

The Twelve Dancing Princesses

Once upon a time there was a king who had twelve beautiful daughters. During the day, the girls were model princesses. But at night, the king didn't know what they got up to. It was very puzzling, because although he carefully locked the door to their room, by morning all their shoes were worn out as if they had been out dancing all night long.

Buying new shoes for his twelve princess daughters was costing the king a lot of money, and he was getting annoyed.

The king announced that whoever discovered where the twelve princesses danced at night could choose his favorite for his bride.

Before long, twelve noble princes took up the challenge. Each one sat guard, in a chair, beside a princess's bed. But before the clock struck twelve, the princes were all asleep. When they awoke in the morning, the princesses had clearly been dancing, because their shoes were full of holes. And so the twelve princes left the kingdom empty-handed.

One day, a poor soldier was passing through the forest near the castle, when he met an old woman who lived there. "Where are you going?" she asked the soldier.

"I thought I'd go and find out where the princesses dance each night," he explained.

"I see," cackled the old woman. "Well, that shouldn't be too hard. But make sure you don't drink anything those princesses offer you." Then she gave him a cloak. "As soon as you put this on you will be invisible," she explained. "That way, you will be able to follow the princesses without their knowing it."

131

So the poor soldier went to the castle to try his luck. That night, as he prepared to sit guard, the eldest princess brought him a glass of water. Remembering the old woman's warning, the soldier threw the water away. Then he sat back and pretended to snore.

When the princesses heard his snores, they started to dress. After they'd pulled on the new shoes that the king had bought that very day, they checked that the soldier was still sleeping. Satisfied that the sleeping potion she had given him had worked, the eldest princess went to her bed and clapped her hands.

The soldier, who was peeking through half-closed eyes, was amazed to see the bed sink into the floor, and a trap door swing open. He watched quietly as each of the princesses went through the trap door one by one.

When the last princess had disappeared, the soldier leaped to his feet, threw the cloak around his shoulders, and became invisible.

Thinking that there wasn't a moment to lose, he raced down the stairs so fast that he stepped on the youngest princess's dress.

"Someone has hold of my gown," cried the princess. But the other princesses told her not to be silly and hurried her along.

At the bottom of the stairs, the soldier followed the princesses through a door into beautiful woodland. The silver leaves on the trees sparkled so brilliantly that the soldier decided to break one off and take it home.

"What was that?" asked the youngest princess. "I'm sure someone is following us."

The other princesses told her not to be silly and hurried her along.

At the edge of the wood, they came to a lake. At the side of the lake lay twelve boats, with twelve handsome princes waiting beside them. By the time a princess and a prince had gotten into each of the boats, they looked so overloaded that the soldier thought they would sink if he got in too.

He eyed each of the princesses in turn. "Who is the lightest?" he wondered. Finally, he decided that the youngest princess was the lightest by far. But even so, the boat rocked and creaked as he got into it.

Halfway across the lake, the prince rowing the boat with the youngest princess and the invisible soldier complained that it felt heavier than usual. "Have you gained weight?" he asked the princess.

"Don't be silly," said the youngest princess, and she hurried him on his way.

On the other side of the lake was a golden castle. The soldier followed the twelve princes and twelve princesses into the castle, and watched them dance the whole night through.

Then, just before dawn, still covered by his invisible cloak, he followed the princesses home.

When they reached the stairs leading to their bedroom, the soldier overtook them, threw off his cloak, and lay snoring in the chair before any of the princesses had climbed into the room through the trap door.

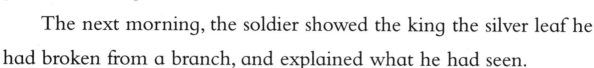

Seeing the soldier still fast asleep, the
princesses thought their secret was safe.

The next morning, the soldier showed the king the silver leaf he
had broken from a branch, and explained what he had seen.

The king was very happy, and asked which of the princesses he
would choose for his bride.

The soldier chose the youngest, whom he thought prettier and
smarter than any of her sisters. She was delighted, for she thought the
soldier even handsomer than her prince.

Shortly after this, the soldier and the princess were married.
Afterward, there was a wonderful ball. The youngest princess danced
with her new husband until midnight.
And as for her eleven sisters? Well,
they danced until dawn!

Shimmer and the River

"How many times have I asked you not to wander off?" said Shimmer the Mermaid's mom, as they swam home from a visit to the surface. "You know you're not allowed to go near the river on the beach."

"Why not?" asked Shimmer. "What's wrong with swimming near the river?"

But Shimmer's mother was in too much of a hurry to answer questions. "Not now, Shimmer," she said impatiently. "Just come along. I'm much too busy to float around arguing with you."

Just then, Swoop the Seagull landed on a large rock nearby.

"YOO-HOO! Swoop, dear!" called Shimmer's mom, flashing through the water with a huge swish of her tail. "I just wanted to have a quick word with you. Do you have a minute?"

"I thought we were in a hurry!" Shimmer muttered, sitting on a ledge. "We'll be here forever now!"

Suddenly the bored little mermaid caught sight of a school of angelfish, darting through the water. "How lovely!" she cried, forgetting all about not wandering off. With a flick of her tail, she swam off to play tag with the multicolored fish. In and out of the rocks they darted, chasing through underwater archways as they went.

Just when Shimmer had almost caught up with them, the school turned in a flash and disappeared into a cave.

"You can't escape!" laughed Shimmer, following them. "I know you're in here!" But there was no sign of the glittering fish. Shimmer swam deeper and deeper down the cave's tunnels, searching for her friends. "Stop hiding!" she called, her voice echoing around.

Shimmer began to feel a little worried. It was dark in the tunnel, and there was no sign of anyone at all.

"I think I'd better turn back," she said to herself, remembering her mother's warnings. "But which way do I go?" Shimmer tried first one tunnel, then another, but none of them seemed to lead in the direction of home. She was lost!

"I'll just have to choose one tunnel and go for it!" she decided, swimming down one that seemed a little brighter than the rest. "This one has to come out somewhere!"

Shimmer had been swimming for what seemed like ages, when she began to notice something strange. As the light at the end of the tunnel got brighter, the water began to get warmer—and it tasted kind of funny, too. There was no salt in it!

Finally, she popped out at the end of the tunnel in a large still pool. Shimmer rubbed her eyes in amazement. This pool was like no other she had ever seen. There was no yellow sand or seaweed in sight. Instead, the edge of the silver pool was soft velvety green, with strange plants growing all around it.

"I must have come out in the river!" she gasped, gazing around her. "How beautiful it all is. I wonder why we're not allowed to come here!"

Just then, Shimmer heard a loud cough and turned around to see a large green frog sitting on a nearby rock. "You're very unusual for a fish!" it croaked.

"But I'm not a fish!" exclaimed Shimmer in surprise. "I'm a mermaid. I live in the ocean!"

"In the ocean!" exclaimed the frog, grinning from ear to ear. "How wonderful to meet someone from the OCEAN!" Then he gave a very loud croak. Slowly, all sorts of woodland creatures began to peek out from behind the bushes to say hello.

"They ran and hid when they first saw you," chuckled the frog. "We've never seen a mermaid before! Please tell us all about life in the ocean!"

So Shimmer began to describe her home to the animals.

She told them about the games of tag she played with the fish, about the friendly dolphins, the grumpy crabs and lobsters, about the beautiful coral reef and the sea anemones that lived on it.

She was so busy talking to her new friends that she didn't notice a shadow swooping over the pond. Suddenly, there was a loud splash as Swoop the Seagull landed in the water beside her.

"Thank goodness I've found you!" squawked the gull. "We must leave immediately! Hurry! I will show you the shortcut back to the ocean."

"It's not fair! " said Shimmer angrily. "I don't want to go home yet. I bet Mom sent you to get me!"

Swoop looked very serious. "She did," he said. "And it's a very good thing she did. Mermaids get sick if they stay in water without salt for too long. If you don't believe me, look at your scales!"

Sure enough, Shimmer's once-glittering scales were colorless and dull.

"I'm sorry, Swoop!" apologized Shimmer, looking shamefaced. "I didn't mean to cause so much trouble. From now on I'll try to listen to what Mom says. It's just that I've made lots of new friends here, and now I won't be able to keep in touch with them!"

Swoop thought carefully for a moment. "Don't worry!" he squawked. "I can deliver messages for you. I often pass this way."

Shimmer and the woodland animals were delighted at the suggestion. "We can send each other news by Seagull Express!" laughed Shimmer, waving goodbye to her new friends. Then, with a flick of her tail, she disappeared beneath the water and headed back to the salty ocean, where mermaids belong.

The Tinderbox

A long time ago, a poor soldier was returning from the war when he met an old woman in the forest.

"You look like a man in need of riches," cackled the old woman. "I can help you."

"How?" asked the poor soldier.

"Take my apron and climb into that hollow tree over there," said the old woman. "You will find a staircase leading down to a cave where there are three doors leading into rooms. In the first room you will find a dog with eyes the size of saucers guarding a chest full of copper coins. In the second you will find a dog with eyes the size of dinner plates guarding a chest full of silver.

"And in the third room you will find a dog with eyes the size of cartwheels guarding a chest full of gold. If you place each dog on my apron they will sit quietly as you help yourself to their treasures."

"Sounds great," cried the soldier, climbing into the tree.

"But wait," cried the old woman. "All I ask in return is that you bring me an old tinderbox you will find there."

The soldier quickly agreed. What could an old tinderbox be worth? After all, a tinderbox was only used to spark a flame, a little like matches are used nowadays.

Soon the soldier found himself in a cave deep beneath the tree. As the old woman had said, there were three doors to choose from. The soldier threw open the first door and entered a room guarded by a dog with eyes the size of saucers.

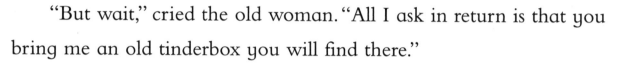

Though the dog was kind of scary, the soldier was a brave man and felt little fear as he placed it on the old woman's apron. The dog was calm as the soldier opened the chest and filled one pocket with copper coins.

Then the soldier moved to the second room. This room was guarded by a dog with eyes the size of dinner plates. Once again, the soldier felt little fear as he placed the dog on the apron and filled his other pocket with silver coins.

Next he moved on to the third room. When he saw the dog with eyes the size of cartwheels, he couldn't help feeling a moment's fear. But quickly he placed the dog on the apron. Then he lifted the lid of the chest and was amazed to find more gold than he'd ever dreamed of. The soldier threw out the copper and silver coins and filled his pockets with gold.

The soldier found the tinderbox, and climbed back up the staircase to where the old woman was waiting.

"For being so honest, I will let you have the tinderbox as well as the coins," cackled the old woman. And with that she disappeared.

The soldier slipped the tinderbox into his bag and thought no more of it as he continued his journey.

Before long, he reached a fine town and found himself a grand house in which to live. No one would have known that he was just a poor soldier. He soon made many friends and he spent his money freely.

One day, one of the soldier's new friends told him about a beautiful princess who was locked within the palace walls.

"No one but the king and queen can visit her," explained the friend. "It has been foretold that she will marry a poor soldier, and her parents don't want her to meet such a man."

The soldier wanted to meet the princess, but he did not see how he could, so he put the idea out of his head.

He continued to live a fine life, until he awoke one morning to find that all his money had been spent. After that, he had to move into a tiny shack.

One night, as he sat in his shack wishing that he had something to light his candle with, he remembered the tinderbox. He took it out, opened it, and struck once with the flint. Immediately, the dog with eyes the size of saucers appeared. He struck a second time, and the dog with eyes the size of dinner plates appeared. He struck a third time, and the dog with eyes the size of cartwheels appeared.

"What can we do for you, master?" roared the dogs.

The soldier asked them to bring him all the copper, silver, and gold they could. And so he was rich once more.

Back in his grand house, the soldier continued his fine life, although sometimes he couldn't help feeling lonely.

One night, when he looked at the tinderbox, he had an idea. He took out the flint and struck once. Immediately, the dog with eyes the size of saucers appeared.

"I wish to see the princess," explained the soldier. And before he had time to say any more, the dog had disappeared and returned with the sleeping princess. She was so beautiful that the soldier kissed her hand. Then the dog returned her to the palace.

The next morning, the princess told the king and queen that she had dreamed about riding on the back of a giant dog, and being kissed on the hand by a handsome soldier.

"Doesn't sound like a dream," thought the queen. That night she made a servant watch over the princess.

Again, the soldier sent the dog to fetch the princess. But this time the servant followed and saw the dog take the princess into the soldier's house.

The servant made a white cross on the door so that in the morning she would be able to show the queen where it was.

But when the dog took the princess home he saw the cross on the door, and marked crosses on every door in town.

There was no way that the queen could find the house in the morning. But she did not give up. She tied a bag to the princess's waist, filled it with sand, and snipped a hole in it.

That night, when the dog carried the princess to the soldier's house, he did not notice the trail of sand he left behind.

The next day, the king and queen quickly found the soldier.

"Do you have a last wish before we fling you into prison?" asked the king.

"Just that you allow me to smoke one last pipe," replied the soldier.

The king could not refuse such a request, so the soldier took out his tinderbox and struck the flint three times. In a flash, the three giant dogs appeared before him.

"Save me!" cried the soldier.

The dog with eyes the size of cartwheels stood guard over the king and queen, while the other two carried the soldier and the princess to a faraway kingdom.

As luck would have it, this kingdom didn't have a king and queen of their own, so when its people saw the princess and her golden crown, they insisted that she become their queen. And, of course, the princess insisted that the soldier become her king!

Rollie the Giant

Rollie was a giant, but he wasn't like other giants. All his giant friends were only happy when they were having a rip-roaring good time, but all Rollie wanted was to quietly do nice things for people.

He liked helping his giant friends, but what made Rollie happiest was doing good deeds for the little people who lived in the village beneath his mountain home. The villagers loved him—as long as he was careful where he stepped, for he was taller than their tallest house. So, provided he tiptoed everywhere, and didn't step on their gardens or lean on their houses, and didn't BOOM around the place the way other giants did, they loved to have him wandering through the village, helping them here and helping them there.

You have no idea how helpful a really helpful giant can be. He plowed the fields by raking his powerful fingers through the soil. He cleared the snow in the winter by scooping it up in big handfuls and patting it firmly onto the side of his mountain. He helped build and repair houses; the villagers never had to hire a crane to fix their roofs—Rollie just lifted up the old roof and carefully lowered the new one into place.

He helped them harvest their apples in the fall, and scatter their seeds in the spring. He gave them rides on his massive shoulders, and helped them search for missing sheep. There was nothing he wouldn't do for people.

The villagers thought Rollie was wonderful and often gave him human food in return for all his hard work. For if there was one thing that made Rollie almost as happy as helping people, it was eating human food. So, all in all, Rollie was a very contented giant.

In fact, there was only one thing that made Rollie the Giant unhappy—the annual Giants' Gathering. The Giants' Gathering was a big, big party, where giants had lots to eat and drink and were awarded glittering prizes.

"It is going to be the same this year," he told the village blacksmith, on the day before the Gathering was to be held on the other side of the mountain, in Gigantia. "All the other giants will be presented with lots and lots of awards, but I won't get a thing. I suppose it's because I don't do anything clever or special."

The next day, Rollie joined all the other giants at the Giants' Gathering. He laughed, clapped, and cheered as the Chief Giant presented each one of his giant friends with an award.

There were awards for running, jumping, throwing, and swimming. There were lots of awards for being smart. There was one for the giant who gave the wildest, noisiest parties. There was even one for the fiercest roaring: "FEEE...FI...FO...FOO...

I WILL SCARE THE PANTS OFF YOU!"

Just as in other years, Rollie was not given an award. When the very last award had been handed out, and all the other giants were leaning out of their seats and patting each other on the back, Rollie couldn't help feeling sad and left out of things.

"Ah, well," he thought, "that's the end for another year." But it wasn't the end at all!

"I would like your attention please!" announced the Chief Giant, just as Rollie was getting ready to go home. "Every year we meet at the Giants' Gathering and have a wonderful time..."

153

"Hear, hear!" cried all the giants. The Chief Giant held up his hand. The hall fell silent.

"We give awards for many different things, but one award we have never presented in all the years I have been Chief Giant is the one for the greatest talent of all… We have never awarded a prize for just being kind and helpful. Well, this year we are going to present such an award."

The Chief Giant stepped forward to the edge of the stage and announced, in his loudest announcing voice:

"IT WILL COME AS NO SURPRISE TO ANY OF YOU THAT THE WINNER FOR BEING THE KINDEST GIANT IN ALL THE WORLD IS… ROLLIE!"

The hall went wild. "Good old Rollie!" everyone cried. "Hooray for Rollie!"

Everyone rose to their feet, clapping and cheering. Rollie stumbled out of his seat and began the long walk to the stage. Tears of pride sprang to his eyes. The Chief Giant smiled and shook his hand.

"Your gift for kindness is so great that the people who live in the village below your mountain have made you a special surprise." Rollie wiped away a tear as a crowd of his tiny village friends appeared on the stage pushing the most enormous cake he had ever seen. Rollie beamed with happiness. His wonderful friends had made him the human food he liked best of all!

"For he's a jolly good fellow…" they began, and they didn't stop singing until the whole cake was gone. Which wasn't very long, because, being such a kind giant, Rollie insisted that everyone had a slice!

The Little Fir Tree

Deep in the forest grew a little fir tree. He was a very pretty fir tree, but he was not happy. He hated being so small and wished he was as tall as the trees who towered above him.

"Oh, if only I was tall, like you," he said to an oak. "Then I'd be able to look out over the world, and birds would nest in my branches."

"Your time will come," said a friendly stork. "Why don't you enjoy being young? Just look how the sun warms you, and the birds and animals play around you."

But the little fir tree refused to listen. Instead, he dreamed of things yet to come.

One day woodcutters came and cut down the tallest trees.

"Where are they going?" the little fir tree asked.

"Ah," squawked the stork. "I've seen trees like that sailing the seven seas, because they have been made into the masts of ships."

Well, the little fir tree thought being a mast and sailing the seven seas sounded much better than hanging out in a boring old forest. After that, he spent so much time dreaming of a life at sea that he barely noticed when summer turned to fall, then fall to winter.

Christmas drew near and men came to dig up the tallest fir trees and take them away.

"Where are they taking them?" the little fir tree asked the stork.

"Ah," squawked the stork. "They are taken into people's houses and decorated with balls and ribbons."

The little tree trembled with excitement. "Oh, that sounds even better than sailing the seven seas. That's what I want to do."

Another year passed, and the little fir tree grew taller and stronger. Christmas came once more, and men came to dig up trees.

"Pick me! Pick me!" cried the little fir tree. Of course, the men couldn't hear him, but because the little fir tree was so handsome he was the first to be dug up.

"Bye-bye," he shouted to his friends, as he was carted away.

Despite the bumpy road, the little fir tree enjoyed his ride into town. However, he was pleased when the cart pulled up outside a fine house and he was lifted off the cart. A man, a woman, and two children came out of the house.

"Isn't it handsome," cried the woman.

"Isn't it tall," cried the man.

"Isn't it pretty," cried the children.

The little fir tree trembled with pride as he was taken into the house and stood in a wooden bucket.

"So this is my new home," he thought. "It's so much grander than the forest. And my new friends say the nicest things."

The little fir tree thought he would burst with happiness when the children came and decorated him. And when the man placed a gold star on his highest tip, he felt like the smartest little fir tree that had ever lived.

The next day was even better. First, the children sat around him to open their presents. Then there was singing and dancing. Oh, how the little fir tree wished he could join in.

In the evening, the children sat around the little fir tree while their father told them wonderful stories. The little fir tree had never heard such tales. It really was the best day of his life.

Long after everyone had gone to bed, the fir tree shook with glee. He couldn't believe what an important little tree he was, nor could he wait to see what happened tomorrow.

Early next morning, the little fir tree stood ready for action. He waited and waited, but nobody came. Then he heard footsteps and voices.

"We'd better get that tree out of here before it starts dropping needles," said the woman.

"Come on, children. Let's take it out," said the man. They picked up the fir tree and carried it from the room.

"Let's put it in the shed," said the man.

It was very quiet and very dark in the shed. The little fir tree didn't like it one bit. He was left there for days and days, and had nothing to do but think.

"I miss the forest," thought the fir tree. "I had so many nice friends there. I wish I could go back."

One day, the shed door swung open. The children had come in search of their sleds. "Hey, it's the Christmas tree," cried the little girl.

"Let's take it into the garden and plant it," said the little boy.

"What now?" thought the fir tree, as he was dragged from the shed and planted in the ground.

At first it felt cold to be outside once more, but as the sun warmed his trunk and birds rested in his branches, the fir tree began to glow with happiness.

A large bird landed beside the fir tree. "So this is where you got to. I've missed you." It was the stork.

The little fir tree trembled with excitement. This was the life—outside, where a fir tree really belonged!

Harry's Grandma, the Pirate

Harry loved playing pirates! He would dress up in pirate's clothes and get his grandma to chase him all round the yard while he shouted, "Shiver m' timbers!" at the top of his voice.

Grandma loved playing with Harry, but she couldn't help feeling just the tiniest bit embarrassed when people saw her pretending to be a pirate. After all, it just wasn't the sort of thing that grandmas usually did.

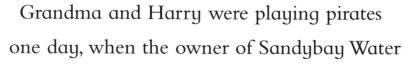

Grandma and Harry were playing pirates one day, when the owner of Sandybay Water Park walked by. Harry and Grandma turned bright red with embarrassment. They were sure that he was going to laugh at Grandma for pretending to be a pirate. But they were wrong.

"My goodness, you are a very good pirate," said the owner of Sandybay Water Park, and he asked Grandma if she would become a full-time pirate on the pretend pirate ship in the water park.

"Oh, I'm not sure," began Grandma. But when she saw how excited Harry was, she quickly agreed.

From then on, she dressed up as a pirate every day and went to Sandybay Water Park to entertain children on the pirate ship.

Sometimes Harry went with her to help. At first Grandma was a little embarrassed when she had to climb up the mast and shout, "Step right up! Come and visit the best pirate ship ever."

But after a few days, she began to enjoy herself.

163

Children rushed to the lake to see the pirate ship. They laughed at Harry's grandma when she swished her sword through the air. They laughed when she strode around the ship's deck, roaring, "Yo, ho, ho, and a bottle of rum."

Harry thought it was great the way his grandma made everyone laugh. And he laughed louder than anyone else.

But they all stopped laughing when some big boys from Sandybay untied the ropes holding the ship to the harbor wall, and the pretend pirate ship sailed out into the lake, taking Grandma, Harry, and all the children with it.

"Stop! Stop!" cried the moms and dads from the side of the lake.

"Help! Help!" shouted the children.

"Go on, Grandma," said Harry, "take the ship back to the harbor."

"But I don't know how!" whispered Grandma.

"Oh, Grandma," said Harry, "you've got to do something!"
Of course, Grandma wasn't really a pirate, and
she didn't really know how to sail a pirate ship.
So she handed out life jackets instead.

Poor Grandma. Poor Harry. Poor children. They
all ran around the deck, pulling this rope and
tugging that rope. But none of them knew how
to turn the ship around, or how to sail it back to
the harbor. And so the ship sailed on and on.

After a while, Grandma was so out of
breath from all the running around that she had
to stop for a rest. She looked over the ship's side.
The waves were very small, the lake was very
blue, the sun was shining, and there was
hardly a cloud in the sky.

"You know," she decided,
"it's a really nice day to
go sailing."

The children looked over
the side of the ship. "It is a
nice day for sailing!" they
quickly agreed.

"Jib-booms and bobstays!" cried Grandma. "Let's have a party."

All the children thought that was a brilliant idea.

"We'll have a picnic," said Grandma. From the ship's kitchen she got a giant bag full of jam tarts, and another bag bulging with sausage rolls. Grandma made some tea. Harry made sandwiches with cheese and tomatoes. One of the children wanted to hard-boil eggs from the ship's storeroom, but Grandma said the eggs had been on board so long that they were bound to be bad; so they put them back, being careful not to break them because bad eggs are terribly smelly.

When everything was ready, they all sat cross-legged on deck and had a feast.

It was such a good one, and everybody enjoyed themselves so much, that no one except Harry noticed that the little ship was sailing into the bay of a sandy island.

"Grandma," said Harry, "we've reached land."

"Land ahoy!" cried Grandma, scrambling to her feet.

"There's a sandy beach," shouted the excited children.

"There'll be pirate's treasure, me hearties!" roared Grandma.

"Excuse me, but there's another pirate ship over there," said one of the children.

And there was! Anchored in the very same bay was another pirate ship, teeming with big boys dressed as pirates.

167

"It's the boys from Sandybay Sailing Club!" said Grandma, "And they're all dressed as pirates."

"Yippee!" shouted the children. "We can have a real pirate fight!"

"They're hoisting the Jolly Roger," laughed Grandma, as a skull and cross-bones flag rose to the top of the other pirate ship's mast.

"Prepare for battle!" cried the biggest boy from the other pirate ship. You could tell he was the captain, because he wore a captain's hat, just like Grandma's.

"They're going to attack us!" laughed a little girl.

The next moment, a bunch of slimy seaweed landed on the deck beside Harry's grandma.

"Hooray! They're firing at us!" shouted Harry.

"Let's fire back," said one of the children. "If we don't do something fast we're going to be covered in seaweed, and then we'll all stink."

"Stink!" cried Grandma. "That's it, we'll make a stink! Children, get all the bad eggs from the ship's storeroom."

When all the eggs had been gently laid on deck, Grandma picked up the biggest and flung it at the big boys' pirate ship. It exploded on the deck in a splash of yellow yolk.

"Bull's-eye! Take that, you sea dogs!" cried Grandma.

"Phooey!" one of the big boys cried.

"Yuck, what a stink!" yelled another.

"Phew! Throwing bad eggs isn't fair," shouted the boy captain.

With their bandannas over their mouths, all the children were soon throwing eggs onto the other pirate ship.

The smell got so bad that all of the boy pirates threw down their seaweed so that they could cover their noses.

"We give up, we give up,"
spluttered the boy captain, who was
gripping his nose so tightly that he
sounded as though he had a bad cold.
"Please let us come aboard so we can
get away from this disgusting smell!"

Grandma allowed all the big boys to
climb aboard. Then she asked everyone what
they should do with them.

"We could hang them all from the top of the mast," suggested one
little boy in a quiet voice.

"Oh, no, they're much too heavy," laughed Grandma.

"We could throw them to the sharks,"
suggested a little girl.

"There are no sharks around
here," laughed the boys.

"Ummm, what can
we do, then?" asked
Grandma.

Harry stood on tiptoe to whisper in her ear.

"Well, I don't know," she said, peering down at him.

"Please, Grandma!" begged Harry.

"Oh, all right," she finally agreed. She turned to the biggest boy. "Would you mind walking the plank?" she asked. "After all, that's a real pirate punishment."

The boy pirates thought that sounded like an excellent idea.

So they blindfolded the boy captain and were about to make him walk the gangplank.

"Don't make me jump," giggled the boy captain, who really thought that it would be loads of fun to jump into the lake.

"Oh, all right," said Grandma, who didn't really think that making someone jump into the lake was a very nice thing to do. "But you must do something. After all, if I were a real pirate I'd make sure you were punished."

"Oh, please make me jump in," cried the boy captain.

But Grandma wouldn't agree.

Suddenly, Harry had another bright idea. He whispered in Grandma's ear.

"What a great idea," cried Grandma. She turned to the boy captain. "You can teach me how to sail. Then I can take the children back to the water park."

Of course the boy captain, who was really the captain of Sandybay Sailing Club, quickly agreed. After all, if there was one thing he loved better than pretending to be a pirate, it was teaching people to sail.

Harry's grandma was such a good pirate that she learned to sail in not much longer than it takes a pirate to flick his pigtail.

"Thank you," she shouted to the big boys as she steered out of the bay.

There had been tremendous panic at Sandybay Water Park

ever since the pretend pirate ship had sailed away. And as Grandma sailed into harbor, a huge crowd, including the park's owner, was waiting.

As the owner frowned at Grandma and looked as if he was going to say something angry, the children all looked at each other and began to cheer.

"Three cheers for good old Harry's grandma!" they cried. "Three cheers for the best and bravest pirate ever to sail the seven seas!"

"Hip, hip, hooray! Hip, hip, hooray! Hip, hip, hooray!"

"Good old Grandma!" shouted the owner of Sandybay Water Park.

"Thank you for looking after our children," shouted the moms and dads.

Harry was so proud of his grandma.

"Shiverme timbers!" he declared. "You're the best grandma in the world."

"And you're the best grandson a pirate could wish for," smiled Grandma.

173

The Golden Goose

Once upon a time, there was a woodcutter who lived with his wife and their three sons. The two oldest sons were clever, and spoiled by their parents. But the youngest, who was called Dan, wasn't so clever or spoiled. Indeed, his mother, father, and brothers laughed at him.

One day the woodcutter was unable to work in the forest, so he sent the eldest son in his place. His mother, who loved her eldest son dearly, packed him a fine lunch of sausage rolls and lemonade and waved goodbye to him.

Before starting work, the eldest son, who was a lazy boy, thought it would be a good idea to have a little bite to eat. So he sat down on a log and laid out the fine food his mother had packed for him. But before he had time to take a bite, an odd little man popped out of nowhere.

"Share your food with a hungry beggar?" asked the man, licking his lips and rubbing his hands together.

"Go away!" snapped the eldest son, who was mean as well as lazy. "This is my food, and I'm not sharing it with anyone, especially a funny little thing like you."

"Well really," said the little man. "Nothing good will come from being so greedy and mean." And, do you know, that's just what the eldest son found out for himself when, after finishing all the sausage rolls and swigging all the lemonade, he cut himself badly and had to go straight home without any wood.

The next day, the middle son was sent to cut wood in his brother's place. Once again, his mother packed a fine lunch for him. Once again, as he sat down to eat, the funny little man popped out of nowhere and asked for a nibble. And, because the middle son was no kinder than his brother, the little man was again told to go away. Which was a mistake, because the middle son also cut himself badly and had to go straight home without any wood. For you see, the little man was a magician.

On the third day, the woodcutter had no choice but to send his youngest son, Dan, to cut wood in the forest. This time, the mother couldn't be bothered to pack a fine lunch, for she considered that anything nice was wasted on her youngest and (in her opinion) silliest son. So she gave him nothing more than a crust of stale bread and a bottle of sour milk and told him he was lucky to get anything at all.

This time, when the little man popped up to ask for a bite to eat, Dan said, "I am afraid it is a very simple meal, but you are more than welcome to share it with me. I always like making new friends."

So, you can imagine his surprise when he unwrapped the food to discover that the tiny scrap of stale bread and the bottle of sour milk had magically turned into yummy sausage rolls and lemonade. Dan and the little man ate and drank until they could eat and drink no more.

"You've been fine company, and I always say that one good turn deserves another," said the little man. "So why don't you cut down that old tree over there? I do believe you will find something interesting beneath it."

Dan chopped down the tree, and do you know what he found beneath it? A goose with feathers of gold!

"Wow!" Dan exclaimed, and turned to thank the little man. But he had vanished.

Dan knew that if he took the golden goose home his brothers would take it away from him. So instead of going home, he decided to walk the world in search of his fortune.

After his first day's traveling, Dan found an inn where he could stay for the night. The innkeeper and his three daughters would have stolen the golden goose from Dan—but he never let it out of his sight, not for a single minute.

The next morning, Dan plucked a golden feather from the goose and paid for his room and board with it. Then he tucked the goose under his arm and left. As the landlord's eldest daughter watched him walk down the road, she thought, "Hmm! Just one of those feathers of gold would buy me a very fine dress indeed." So she raced after Dan and reached out to pluck a feather from the goose's tail. But, do you know, as soon as she touched the goose, she couldn't let go.

"Let me go! Let me go!" screamed the girl.

But Dan just strode on, saying, "I can't stop now. I've got a whole world to explore."

So the girl screamed and shouted, until her sisters came out to see what the commotion was about. They grabbed hold of their eldest sister and tried to pull her away. But as soon as they touched her, they, too, were stuck fast.

Dan strode on, ignoring the girls' cries. Then, as they were passing though the village, the parson saw what he thought were three girls chasing a boy. "Disgraceful behavior!" he cried, and caught hold of the girls to pull them away. But, as I am sure you have guessed, as soon as he touched the last girl in the line, he was stuck fast.

179

And so it went on and on, until Dan and his goose had quite a following. There were the landlord's three daughters, the parson, a schoolteacher, a village blacksmith, a bellringer, four shopkeepers, thirteen housewives… Together they marched on and on until they reached the city where the king lived.

Dan had heard that the king had a daughter who, though very beautiful, was always sad and never laughed. This made the king so unhappy that he had promised her hand in marriage to whoever made her laugh.

Dan was used to making people laugh without even trying, so he was sure that he could bring a smile to the princess's face.

Boldly, he marched right up to the palace, and into the courtyard. You should have seen how people pointed and laughed to see Dan and his golden goose being followed by such a long line of struggling people.

They laughed so much that the princess came to see what all the fuss was about. And when she saw Dan and his goose, with the long tail of stumbling, struggling people following close behind him, her lips began to twitch, her chin began to wobble, and, before she knew it, she was roaring with laughter. In fact, it wasn't a very ladylike laugh at all. But the king didn't mind a bit, and he said that Dan and the princess should be married at once.

Dan never forgot the odd little man, and when he eventually became king, he never forgot that "one good turn deserves another."

The Wizard's Test

Long ago, in a castle on a mountain high up in the clouds, there lived a young boy called Joe. Of course, it was no ordinary castle, and Joe was no ordinary boy. The castle was home to a group of good wizards, and Joe was an orphan who had been left on the doorstep as a baby. The kind wizards took him in, and from that day on, Joe lived with them, helping around the castle to earn his keep.

Joe was very happy living with the wizards, but the older he got, the more he longed to become a wizard himself. One day, he finally plucked up enough courage to speak to Magicus, the head wizard.

"I want to become a wizard," he told the kind old man. "What do I have to do to become one?"

Magicus smiled at Joe. "I'm sure you would make a great wizard," he told him. "But before we are allowed to teach anyone our magic secrets, we must be sure that they are trustworthy. You must prove yourself by passing the wizard's test!"

"What's that?" asked Joe.

"You must start by going to the forest on the other side of the mountain," said Magicus. "Then you must find the secret glade at its very heart."

"But what should I do when I get there?" asked Joe.

"I'm not allowed to tell you that," replied Magicus mysteriously. And with that, he disappeared in a swirl of silver magic dust.

Early the next morning, Joe set off down the mountain to find the forest, taking only a hunk of bread and cheese in a knapsack. It was almost noon when he reached the edge of the trees. The forest was strangely quiet when he entered it. Joe suddenly felt frightened.

Joe had heard all sorts of stories about the weird creatures that lived in the forest. "I will be brave," he whispered to himself, as he pushed through the brambles.

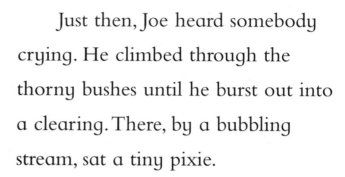

Just then, Joe heard somebody crying. He climbed through the thorny bushes until he burst out into a clearing. There, by a bubbling stream, sat a tiny pixie.

"What's the matter?" cried Joe. "Are you hurt?"

The pixie looked up. "Oh, no!" he sniffed, wiping his nose on his sleeve. "I'm crying because I'm so hungry. I haven't eaten for days."

Joe was reaching into his knapsack for a handkerchief, when suddenly he had an idea. "Here! Take my lunch," he said. "You need it far more than I do!"

The pixie was delighted. "How kind you are!" he cried. "How can I thank you?"

"You could show me the way to the secret glade," suggested Joe.

"Of course," replied the little man. "Just follow the stream and it will lead you there."

"Thank you," said Joe politely, before turning to wave goodbye. But the little pixie had disappeared! All that remained was a swirl of silver dust.

"I wonder where he went!" exclaimed Joe, setting off on his way once again.

Joe had not gone far when he saw something gleaming in the bushes. He knelt down to take a closer look, and gasped in amazement as he pulled out a beautiful crystal ball. It was exactly like the ones in the magic books at the castle. Joe picked it up and gazed at it longingly. "I wish it was mine!" he said. Would it matter if he slipped it into his pocket? It didn't seem to belong to anyone.

Joe was just about to put it in his pocket, when suddenly an old man appeared before him. He seemed to be looking for something. "Are you searching for this?" asked Joe, holding out the crystal ball.

"My precious crystal!" cried the old man happily. "I thought I had lost it forever. What an honest young man! How can I ever thank you?"

"You could help me to find my way to the secret glade," suggested Joe.

"Just follow the water," chuckled the old man, pointing downstream.

Joe turned to thank the man, but he had disappeared in a swirl of silver dust.

"This is a very strange place," muttered Joe, as he set off down the stream once again.

As Joe went deeper into the forest, he had to fight to push his way through the bushes and brambles. The thorns scratched his legs, but he kept going. Then, just as he was about to give up hope of ever finding the secret place, the forest opened out into a cool green glade with a shimmering pond in the middle.

"The secret glade!" cried Joe. "Maybe now I will find out what I have to do for the wizard's test!"

Just then, Magicus appeared in a swirl of silver magic dust. "You have already completed the test!" smiled the wizard. "And I'm pleased to say that you have passed with flying colors!"

"But I haven't done anything yet!" frowned Joe.

"Yes, you have," replied Magicus. "I have been watching you today, disguised as a pixie and an old man. You traveled through the forest even though you were afraid, gave me your food, and returned my crystal ball, even though you longed to keep it. You have proved that you are brave and kind and honest—the three things that every good wizard must be. I have no doubt at all that we can trust a young man like you with ALL our magic secrets. And now, I think it's time I taught you your very first spell—a spell to magic yourself back home to the castle for a special wizard celebration!"

The Swineherd

Once upon a time, there was a poor prince. He was very kind and handsome, and many fine ladies would have been happy to marry him. But the prince only wished to marry the emperor's beautiful daughter. She, however, had other ideas.

"You're much too poor," she said. "You might own a palace and have enough money for an ordinary girl, but you just don't have any gold to keep me in the jewels and gifts I deserve." And with that she pushed him out of her father's palace and told him not to come calling on her again.

The prince might not have been as rich as your average prince, but he had two things much better than gold.

First, he had a rosebush that grew a single rose every five years; its perfume smelled so wonderful that anyone who sniffed it was filled with joy. The second thing was a nightingale whose voice was so sweet that anyone who heard it felt kindness and love.

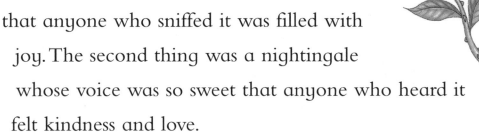

The prince decided to give these two things to the emperor's daughter. He was sure that as soon as she saw them, she would want to become his bride. He packed them in two wooden chests and delivered them himself.

The emperor's daughter opened the first chest. When she took out the rose, she threw it down in disgust.

"It's just a smelly old rose," she cried. Its perfume didn't fill her with joy.

She opened the second chest, and out flew the nightingale. As it began to sing, the emperor and his courtiers clapped their hands with glee. But the emperor's daughter just frowned.

"Why would I want a silly old bird?" she asked, for the nightingale's song didn't fill her with kindness and love.

She had the prince thrown out of her father's palace. "As if I'd marry anyone who gave me such silly gifts," she shouted, throwing the wooden chest out the window.

Although the prince was upset, he still wanted to marry the emperor's daughter.

The next day he dressed as a beggar and called at the palace looking for work.

"I have just the job for you," said the emperor, looking at the prince's ragged clothes. "I need someone to look after my pigs."

So the beggar prince became the royal swineherd. Each morning he tended the pigs, and each afternoon he sat outside his hut making things.

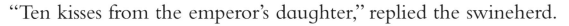

One afternoon he made a silver cooking pot, covered with bells. When the pot boiled, the silver bells tinkled a little tune.

When the emperor's daughter saw the silver pot, and heard the lovely tune it tinkled, she wanted it for herself. She sent her servant to ask the swineherd what he wanted for the pot.

"Ten kisses from the emperor's daughter," replied the swineherd.

The emperor's daughter was furious. "How dare he!" she shouted. But when the bells began to tinkle once more, she marched to where the swineherd sat.

"Very well. You shall have your kisses," she said. "But I don't want to be seen by anyone."

She made a group of servants gather around her, and the swineherd got his ten kisses. He should have been happy, but he couldn't help thinking that the emperor's daughter was spoiled.

The next day, the swineherd made a beautiful golden rattle.

When it was swung in the air it played wonderful tunes.

"I must have it," said the emperor's daughter. Once again, she sent her servant to find out what the swineherd wanted for it.

"One hundred kisses from the emperor's daughter," he replied.

After a little protest, the emperor's daughter agreed. Once again, she made her servants gather around while she kissed the swineherd. As the servants counted the kisses, the swineherd couldn't help thinking that perhaps the emperor's daughter was too spoiled and greedy to make a good wife.

But before he had time to say anything, the emperor, who happened to be walking by, spotted the gaggle of servants gathered in a circle around the swineherd's hut.

"What's going on here?" he demanded. As you can imagine, he was furious when he discovered that his daughter was being kissed by the swineherd.

"How dare you," he shouted, and immediately had his daughter and the swineherd thrown out of the palace.

The emperor's daughter stamped her foot and cried.

"If only I'd married the handsome prince who gave me the rose and the nightingale," she wailed.

The swineherd disappeared for a moment, then reappeared dressed as a prince.

The prince looked sadly at the emperor's daughter. "I'm sorry," he said, "but I don't think I can marry you. You are just too silly. After all, you didn't want my lovely rose and nightingale, but were willing to kiss a swineherd for the sake of a few glittering trinkets."

Then, with a sad farewell, he went back to his own little kingdom.

And as for the emperor's daughter? Well, her father eventually let her back into the palace. But only after she'd promised never to be quite so silly again!

Thoroughly Messy Milly

Everyone loved Milly. But everyone had to agree that she was a very messy little girl.

You see, Milly hated brushing her hair and thought that washing was only for very special occasions, like Christmas and birthdays.

"Birds will nest in your hair," teased her dad, as he chased her with a hairbrush. Milly thought that birds nesting in her hair sounded like lots of fun, so she made a quick getaway.

"Toadstools will sprout out of your ears if you don't wash them," joked Mom when Milly ran away at bathtime. But Milly just laughed and told her not to be silly.

But if people thought that Milly was messy, they should have seen her bedroom. You couldn't even see the floor under the toys and books, and the bed was hidden by a pile of clothes.

"You'll get lost in here one of these days," laughed Dad when he came to read her a bedtime story.

"Don't be silly," laughed Milly. "Nobody could get lost in a bedroom."

Later that night, Milly awoke with a jolt. Something was flapping around in her hair. She reached her hand up into the tangled mess and felt something warm and feathery. Goodness! A bird had nested in her hair! It seemed friendly, but Milly thought she'd better tell Mom.

Milly opened her mouth and shouted, "Mom" at the top of her voice, but no sound came out. Suddenly, Milly realized that she couldn't hear anything at all. Not even her hamster, who she could see racing around on his wheel on the other side of the room.

"That's strange," thought Milly, feeling her ears. But, yuck, that was even stranger. Toadstools were growing out of her ears. No wonder she couldn't hear a thing.

"I'd better go get Mom and Dad," thought Milly. "They'll know what to do."

So Milly jumped out of bed and found herself covered in toys, books, and clothes.

"I'm sure I didn't have this much stuff," thought Milly, as she attempted to make her way to the door.

But no matter which way Milly turned, she found her way blocked by toys and other stuff. Meanwhile, the bird kept flapping in her hair and the toadstools in her ears grew larger and larger.

Milly caught sight of her reflection in an old mirror that was propped up against Big Teddy. She was such a terrible mess that she just had to laugh.

"Maybe I'll brush my hair and wash my ears tomorrow," she thought, as she began to burrow under some old books.

"Is this the way to the door?" she asked a broken doll she found lying under the chest of drawers. But, of course, the doll didn't reply.

At last Milly found a doorknob and gave it a yank.

Oops! It wasn't the bedroom door at all. It was the door to the closet. The closet where Milly crammed things when there was nowhere else left to cram them.

"Maybe I should clear you out sometime," she said, as stuffed toys, books, and games poured on top of her.

Milly wandered all around the room, but every way she turned she just found more junk.

The mess in Milly's room seemed to be growing.

"This isn't funny anymore," Milly told Big Teddy, after she'd bumped into him for the third time. "If I ever get out of here, I'll promise not to be messy ever again. Not ever."

Milly dived under a pile of clothes and books and attempted to tunnel her way through the mess to the door.

Suddenly, the light flashed on.

"Milly, what are you doing thrashing around your room? Are you okay?" It was Mom and Dad.

"Help, help!" shouted Milly, emerging from beneath an old jacket. "I'm lost in here. There's so much mess that I can't get out."

"Don't be silly," laughed Dad. He reached down and picked Milly up from under the jacket.

Milly looked down at her room. It looked the same as it usually did. Messy, but not as messy as it had been five minutes ago.

"But what about the bird in my hair and the toadstools in my ears?" whispered Milly.

"What bird? What toadstools?" Dad showed Milly her reflection in the bathroom mirror.

"You must have been dreaming," laughed Mom, and Milly realized she was right.

"Can I take a bath?" asked Milly.

"I must be dreaming," laughed Dad.

After that night, Milly was never messy again. Her hair was always brushed and her skin always sparkled. And as for her room, well, it was the neatest one in the house. After all, it may have been a dream, but you can never be too careful. Can you?

Hansel and Gretel

Once, a long, long time ago, a poor woodcutter lived in the forest with his two children, Hansel and Gretel. The children's real mother had died a long time ago, so when the woodcutter took a new wife they were overjoyed. However, their joy was short-lived, for their new stepmother was a wicked woman who did not like children.

One long winter, there was little food in the woodcutter's house, and everybody went hungry. On one particularly cold night, Hansel and Gretel were so hungry that they could not sleep. As they lay tossing and turning in their beds they overheard their parents talking.

"There's just not enough food to go around," said the wicked stepmother. "Hansel and Gretel will have to go. Tomorrow you must lead them into the forest and leave them there."

"No!" gasped the woodcutter. But the wicked stepmother wouldn't leave him alone until he agreed.

"What shall we do? If we're left in the forest we're sure to be eaten by wild animals," sobbed Gretel.

Hansel sat gazing out the window while he decided what could be done to save them. Then he noticed something that gave him an idea. The moon was shining on some white pebbles, making them stand out like daisies against a green lawn. Hansel crept down to the garden and collected a handful of the pebbles.

Early the following morning, Hansel and Gretel followed the woodcutter deep into the forest. As they walked along, Hansel kept stopping to drop white pebbles on the ground.

After a long walk, they reached a clearing in the middle of the forest. "Wait here," said their father. "I'm going to cut wood. I will be back to fetch you at the end of the day."

Hansel and Gretel waited and waited, but their father never returned.

"We'll never find our own way home," said Gretel as darkness began to fall. But Hansel told her not to worry.

When the moon eventually began to shine, the pebbles that Hansel had dropped stood out just as they had in the garden.

Holding hands, Hansel and Gretel followed the trail of glistening pebbles all the way home. Their father was overjoyed when they walked into the house, but their stepmother was far from pleased.

A few nights later, the children overheard their stepmother talking once more. "Those children really must go, or we will all starve. Tomorrow you must take them even farther into the forest, and this time make sure they can't find their way back."

After much argument, their father reluctantly agreed.

That night, Hansel tried to go out into the garden to collect pebbles, but his stepmother had locked the door. So the next day, instead of dropping pebbles, Hansel dropped breadcrumbs on their journey through the woods.

Once again, their father left them and promised to return before nightfall. Once again, he failed to return.

Hansel and Gretel waited for the
moon to rise, then looked for the trail of
breadcrumbs. But there was not a single
breadcrumb to be seen, for hungry birds
had gobbled them all up.

Hansel and Gretel wandered through the
forest all night long, but they could not find their way home. Then, as
the sun began to rise, they came across a pretty little cottage.

Hansel and Gretel could not believe their eyes, for it was
made of bread, cake, and candy. They were so hungry that
they began to eat bits of the pretty cottage at once.

But before they had eaten more than a few mouthfuls,
the cottage door swung open and
an ugly old witch jumped out—a
witch so wicked that she had built
her delicious house to trap
innocent children.

Cackling with delight, she dragged the children into her cottage and locked Hansel in an iron cage. Then she turned on Gretel. "As for you," she cackled, "you're going to cook things all day long. You're going to cook lots and lots of food and feed it to your scrawny little brother until he is as round and fat as a juicy pig. Then I am going to eat him. And if I am still hungry, I will eat you, too!"

From then on, Hansel was given lots and lots of the very finest food, while Gretel was given nothing but bones to gnaw on. One day, Gretel gave one of the bones to Hansel. "Hold it out to the witch when she asks to feel your finger in order to see how fat you've become," said Gretel. "She is so nearsighted that she will never know the difference."

Clever little Gretel was right, and the witch was astonished that Hansel was so skinny. Then, one day, she grew impatient:

"Fat or thin, I am going to eat him all the same," she cried. "Light the oven, Gretel. Today's the day we make boy pie."

Gretel did as she was told, and soon the fire beneath the oven was blazing. "Is it hot enough yet?" asked the witch.

"I don't know," said Gretel, opening the oven door. "Why don't you look in and see for yourself?"

So the foolish witch stuck her head in the oven and Gretel pushed her in. Then, quick as a flash, she slammed the door shut.

Gretel found the witch's keys and released Hansel. Then they used the keys to open all the chests in the witch's cottage.

Inside they discovered all sorts of
precious jewels. "We will be able
to buy Father all the food we need
with this," laughed Hansel.

When their pockets were filled
with jewels, they set off in search of
their home. This time, they found it
without much difficulty. When their father
saw them he was overjoyed that they had returned.
Quickly they told each other what had happened. The woodcutter
explained that their wicked stepmother was gone, and Hansel and
Gretel told their father all about the wicked witch and the jewels.

From that day on, the woodcutter, Hansel, and Gretel never went
without food again.

The Birthday Surprise

The queen of the fairies' birthday was on Midsummer Day, and the fairies and elves of the forest were busy preparing for the party that evening. Everyone had a job to do. The older ones were making fairy cakes, iced rose petals, and dewdrop candy for the feast, while the youngsters were flitting around in search of acorn cups for the nectar juice. The crickets were practicing their top ten hits for the disco, and Strawberry, the queen's chief elf-in-waiting had spent the whole morning setting out clues for a fairy treasure hunt.

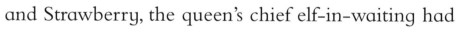

Daffodil, Rose, and Holly were trying to hang a huge banner from the branches of the oak tree, but not with very much success.

"Left a bit, right a bit, up a bit…" called Holly from the forest floor. "No, down a bit, left a bit…"

"For goodness sake, make your mind up!" complained Daffodil, hovering high in the branches of the oak tree. "Our wings are going to drop off soon!"

"That will have to do!" said Rose, fluttering down to the ground. "We've got tons of other chores to do before the party starts. I've still got a hundred honey-coated dreamy-cream puffs to make…"

"And don't forget, we've got to decorate the queen's throne with blossoms," added Holly. "We haven't even picked the flowers yet."

They all looked at each other in dismay. "Oops! I forgot about that," gulped Rose.

209

"We'd better get going right away. I know a glade where there are some beautiful pink roses. We can use those…"

"Not pink again," groaned Holly. "It's always pink, pink, pink with you! Why can't we have green leaves instead?"

"GREEN!" exclaimed Daffodil. "We don't want green leaves, or pink flowers, for that matter. What we need are some sunny yellow flowers for a change."

"That's typical of you two!" cried Rose, beginning to lose her temper. "You never listen to what I want to do."

I'm ashamed to say that Daffodil, Rose, and Holly were soon squabbling like kindergarten fairies.

"GREEN!" cried Holly.

"YELLOW!" yelled Daffodil.

"PINK!" shouted Rose at the top of her voice.

"What on earth is going on?" interrupted a surprised voice. It was Strawberry. He had come to see what all the fuss was about. He listened quietly as the three fairies explained what had started the argument. When they were finished, he shook his head slowly. "There's no need for all this shouting!" he said wisely. "There's only one fair way to settle a question like this. We must hold a pow-wow in the fairy ring."

As Strawberry waved his wand in a circle, tiny red-and-white-spotted mushrooms pushed up through the warm soil to make a perfect ring around them. Then he took a shell from his pocket and blew into it like a horn. The sound of the shell called all the other fairies to the glade, and before long the air was filled with the sound of chattering voices.

Strawberry raised his hands for silence. "I've called a pow-wow so that we can decide what color flowers to use to decorate the queen's throne," he announced. "If you want to suggest a color, you must step into the ring and tell everyone why you have chosen it. At the end of the pow-wow, I will choose the winner."

Holly cleared her throat, then bravely stepped forward into the fairy ring. "Everyone knows that our queen loves the green, green forest," she said, "and that's why I think we should choose the color green."

It was Daffodil's turn next. "The Queen loves golden yellow sunshine," she told the crowd. "That's why I think we should choose yellow."

"Pink is the color of her favorite blossoms," whispered Rose, who felt a little shy in front of everyone.

"Red is the color of summer strawberries," suggested another little fairy, "and the queen loves strawberries. Maybe we should decorate the throne red!"

"The Queen may love strawberries in the summer," announced one fairy confidently, "but juicy purple plums are her favourite in the fall. I think we should choose purple."

"Why don't we choose orange, like the sunset," said someone else. "Her Majesty always says that's the most beautiful time of day."

"You're all wrong!" cried one very excited fairy. "Blue is the color of the sky and the river. You know how the queen loves to lie on the riverbank and gaze at the sky."

Finally, when everyone who wanted to speak had said his or her piece, the glade fell silent. Everyone looked at Strawberry expectantly. Which color would he choose?

But Strawberry didn't give his answer. He just smiled mysteriously. "Rose, Daffodil, and Holly," he said, his eyes sparkling with fun, "come with me. We have work to do. The Queen's throne needs decorating!"

Later that evening, it was amid much excitement that the fairies made their way through the forest to the birthday party. What delicious things would there be to eat? Who would dance with them at the party? And most important, what color would the flowers around the queen's throne be?

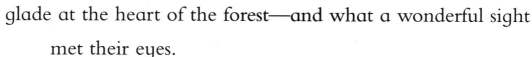

Glowworms lit the way like candles, as the cricket music beckoned the fairies on through the trees. Finally, they emerged into the fairy glade at the heart of the forest—and what a wonderful sight met their eyes.

HAPPY BIRTHDAY

There on the throne sat the queen. Arching around her like a rainbow were flowers of every color.

"Welcome, everyone!" she smiled graciously. "Thank you for my party. And thank you most of all for the beautiful flower decorations.

Strawberry has told me why each color flower was chosen! What a perfect gift for my birthday!"

The fairies of the forest glowed with pride, but no one was more proud than Rose, Daffodil, and Holly.

Beauty and the Beast

Once upon a time there was a rich merchant who lived in a grand house with his three beautiful daughters. The girls were given everything they wanted and were waited on by an army of servants.

The two eldest sisters were very vain and very spoiled, but the youngest, who was also the prettiest, was kind and sweet. Indeed, she was so pretty and kind that everyone called her "Beauty."

All three girls led a fine life and couldn't have been happier. Then one day, disaster struck. Their father lost his fortune, and so they had to move to a tiny cottage in the woods. The two eldest girls were not at all happy and spent every day grumbling and squabbling. But Beauty couldn't have been happier. She loved the little cottage and enjoyed cleaning it and tending its little garden.

And so they settled into their new life, until one day their father was called away on business. It was a trip that promised to help give them back their fortune, so you can imagine how excited everyone was. Before he left, the merchant asked each of his daughters what present she would like him to bring back. The two elder girls reeled off an endless list.

"Pearl necklace… diamond brooch… velvet gown… silk scarves… gold ring…" said one.

"Emerald bracelet… sapphire earrings… silk gown… silver comb… gold slippers…" said the other.

However, when the merchant asked Beauty what she would like, she thought for a moment, then said, "What I would wish for most of all is a single red rose. We have none in our garden, and I do love them so."

This simple request brought a tear to the merchant's eye that stayed with him throughout his long journey.

The trip proved a success, and the merchant traveled home a much richer man. He had bought the dresses and jewels the elder daughters had asked for, and was searching for a red rose for Beauty when he became quite lost.

As night began to fall, the weary traveler looked around for shelter, and was surprised to come across a grand palace hidden deep in the woods. On the palace gates was a bold sign, which read:

WELCOME ALL TRAVELERS

As the merchant approached the gates, they swung open as if inviting him in. The merchant looked around, but no one was there. He shrugged his shoulders in surprise, then hurried to put his horse in the well-kept, but empty, stable. After he had fed and watered the horse, he knocked on the palace door. No one answered, but the palace door swung open.

The merchant wandered through the palace. All the rooms were richly furnished and fires burned in all the grates, but no one was there. In one of the rooms, a tempting meal was laid out on a table. The merchant waited to see if anyone would come, but eventually hunger got the better of him and he sat down to dine alone.

When he had finished eating, the merchant looked around for a place to sleep. In one of the bedrooms, the bed was made, and, remembering the sign on the gate, the merchant spent the night there.

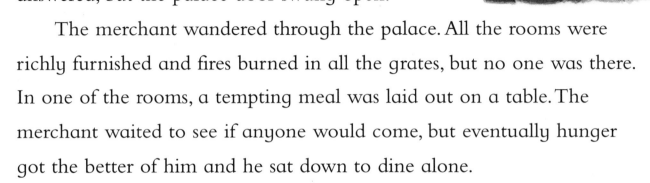

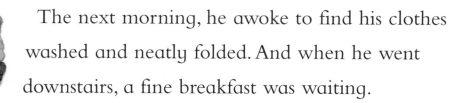

The next morning, he awoke to find his clothes washed and neatly folded. And when he went downstairs, a fine breakfast was waiting.

After breakfast, the merchant decided to take a walk in the garden before leaving. It was a beautiful morning, and the flowers in the garden were beyond compare. As he walked beneath a climbing rose, the merchant remembered Beauty's request and reached up to pluck a single red rose.

As soon as he held the rose in his hand, he heard a terrible roar. Terrified, he turned to find an ugly beast racing toward him.

"How dare you steal my prize rose," snarled the Beast. "Is that how you repay me for letting you stay in my home?"

"But I was just picking the rose for my youngest daughter," began the merchant.

"I don't care," said the Beast. "You will pay heavily for your crime. You will become my prisoner, and never leave this place."

Thinking of his poor daughters, who would surely starve without him, the merchant begged to be let go.

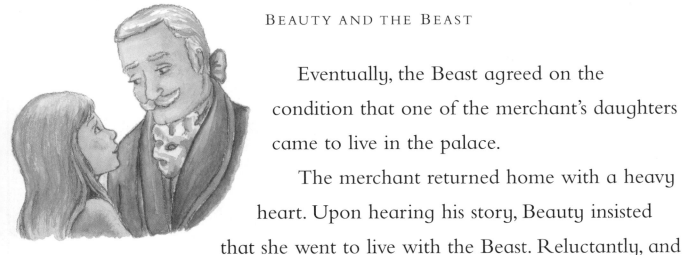

Eventually, the Beast agreed on the condition that one of the merchant's daughters came to live in the palace.

The merchant returned home with a heavy heart. Upon hearing his story, Beauty insisted that she went to live with the Beast. Reluctantly, and after much argument, the merchant finally agreed.

When the merchant took Beauty to the palace, it was just as empty as on his first visit. But after they had eaten a meal, the Beast appeared. Beauty had never seen anything so ugly, but she tried to hide her fear.

"So you have come in your father's place," said the Beast, as gently as he could. "You must love him very much."

"Yes," nodded Beauty, trying not to shrink away.

"You are a kind girl," said the Beast. "I will treat you well."

Seeing that the Beast was so gentle with Beauty, the merchant felt less worried as he returned home.

And so Beauty's new life began. She spent each day alone in the palace, then in the evening was joined by the Beast. In time, Beauty grew fond of the Beast and began looking forward to his company.

At the end of each evening, just before leaving, the Beast would say, "Will you marry me, Beauty?"

And Beauty would always reply, politely, "No thank you, Beast."

Then the Beast would give a heavy sigh, and leave. But the next evening he would ask her again. And again Beauty would reply, "No thank you, Beast."

It made Beauty sad to think that she made the Beast unhappy, but there was no way she could marry such an ugly creature.

Beauty hadn't been living in the palace for very long when she began to feel homesick. When the Beast, who was really very kind and cared greatly for Beauty, realized what was wrong, he gave her an enchanted mirror.

Whenever Beauty looked into the mirror, she could see her family. In this way, she always knew what was happening in her father's house.

Beauty looked into the mirror each day, and each day was pleased to see her family looking happy. They had moved back into their big house and her father's business was doing well. Her sisters, who were as vain as ever, both found husbands and left home. Beauty was pleased for them, but felt sad to think that she would never be a bride.

Then one day, Beauty was feeling particularly homesick. She looked into her mirror to cheer herself up but got a terrible shock. For there was her father, sick in bed, with both of her sisters weeping at his side.

When the Beast came that evening, he saw that something was wrong and asked Beauty what was troubling her. Beauty quickly explained and begged the Beast to let her visit her father.

223

After much thought, the Beast reluctantly agreed to let her go, but he made her promise she wouldn't stay away for long.

The next morning, when Beauty awoke, she found herself not in the Beast's palace but in her father's house. As soon as her father saw her, his heart lifted, and from that day on he began to get better.

Some weeks had passed, and her father had been well for some time, when Beauty remembered her promise to the Beast. She looked into her magic mirror, and was alarmed to see the Beast alone and dying. Immediately, she arranged for her father to take her back to the Beast's palace.

On arriving, she found the Beast lying beneath his beloved climbing rose. "Please don't die," cried Beauty. "I couldn't live without you."

"I thought you'd forgotten all about me and would never come back," said the Beast. "Without you, I had nothing to live for."

"Forgive me," sobbed Beauty. "When I saw that you were ill, I realized that I love you. I will marry you, if you'll still have me."

And as soon as she whispered those words, the Beast changed into a handsome prince!

The prince quickly explained that an evil witch had cast a spell, turning him into a Beast—a spell that could only be broken when somebody loved him and promised to marry him.

Beauty was delighted with her handsome prince, and couldn't wait to tell her father of her good fortune. Not long after, Beauty and the prince were married. And in her hands, Beauty carried a bunch of red roses from the Beast's rosebush.

Monkey Business

There was trouble in the jungle. Someone had stolen Big Baboon's prize melon, and Lion was pretty sure he knew who it was. He decided to pay Monkey a visit.

When Monkey heard Lion coming, he tried to hide the melon behind his back. But the fruit was twice as wide as his skinny little body, and it could be seen very clearly poking out at either side.

Lion's brown eyes flashed with fury.

"Monkey," he roared, "this has to stop! No animal steals from another animal in my part of the jungle. If you keep doing this, I'll banish you."

Monkey was angry, and swung away through the jungle. As he did so, he saw Elephant trundling through the trees with a big pile of bananas on his back. The bananas looked ripe and delicious, and Monkey's mouth watered. But Lion would be furious with him if he stole Elephant's bananas! He had no wish to be banished from the jungle, as Cheetah had been some months before for taking an antelope. What was a monkey to do?

As he wandered moodily along the riverbank, a pair of eyes, a snout, and two ears popped up from out of the water.

"Hello, Monkey," Hippo called in a friendly voice.

Monkey was in no mood for conversation. He ignored her and kept going.

"Ow!" he said suddenly, stubbing a toe on a hollow log that was sticking out of the water. He turned the log over in his hand. It reminded him of something. Of course! It looked exactly like Hippo! He slipped it over his head, gazed at his reflection in the water, and chuckled.

227

He had just had a brilliant idea.

The next morning, when Hippo poked her head above the water, she found Elephant marching up and down the bank.

"Hippo!" trumpeted Elephant. "How dare you steal my bananas! The bush babies saw you sneaking away with them last night!"

"It wasn't me," protested Hippo. "I don't like bananas! Even if I did, my legs are much too short for me to reach the branches!"

But Elephant was in no mood to listen. He stomped off back into the jungle, crushing plants and bushes and making all the little animals skip hastily out of his way.

High up in the mango tree, with the hippo mask at his side, Monkey peeled a banana and chuckled softly to himself.

The next morning, Hippo had a visit from Lion. "Hippo!" he roared. "Crocodile's absolutely furious! Several of the night animals have reported seeing you taking her eggs last night. One more stunt like that, and you're banished from the jungle."

"It wasn't me!" protested Hippo. "I was asleep all night. Besides, I hate crocodile eggs!" she added sulkily. But Lion had already stalked back into the bushes.

High up in the mango tree, Monkey cracked open an egg and chuckled to himself.

The next day, Lion called a meeting. "We have a problem," he told the animals gravely. "Cheetah has returned to the jungle."

A murmur of fear spread through the crowd of animals.

"As you know," Lion continued, "nobody's safe when Cheetah's around. You will all have to be extra careful."

While Lion was speaking, Monkey dozed in his tree. His midnight raids had worn him out.

Later that night, Monkey put on his hippo log-mask and set off through the jungle. He chuckled when he spotted Ostrich fast asleep at the edge of the trees. Silly bird! She'd get a real shock when she found her tail feathers missing in the morning!

As Monkey sneaked toward Ostrich, another animal prowled through the long grass from the opposite direction. The grass was so long that Monkey did not see Cheetah, and Cheetah did not see Monkey until they were almost on top of each other.

BUMP!

As the two animals crashed into each other, Ostrich woke up with a great squawk, while Monkey let out a frightened little yelp. The little yelp echoed and rumbled inside the hollow mask, so that when it came out it had turned into a big, deep, booming ROOOOARRR!

It was all too much for Cheetah. While Monkey bounded back into the trees, Cheetah tucked her tail between her legs and fled, never to return to that part of the jungle.

The next day, the news spread like wildfire. Hippo had saved Ostrich and scared Cheetah away single-handed!

Lion led all the animals down to the riverbank.

"Hippo!" he called. "Are you there?"

At the sight of the lion, zebra, giraffe, snake, antelope, and elephant lined up along the bank, Hippo's heart sank. She thought about diving down to the bottom of the riverbed and staying there, but decided that she might as well get it over with.

"Yes, Lion," she said in a small voice.

"Hippo," said Lion, "Ostrich has told us how you scared Cheetah away last night. You are the bravest animal in the jungle."

"But Lion..." began Hippo.

"Not another word," said Lion, holding up his great paw.

All day long and late into the night, the animals sang songs about Hippo's bravery, and promised to bring her the finest food the jungle had to offer every day for the rest of her life.

Monkey stared down from his branch high up in the mango tree. He didn't feel like chuckling at all.

The Spring Unicorn

Far away, beyond the widest oceans, lies the enchanted land of Faria. The people of Faria are always happy, for the summers are long, the falls are beautiful, the springs are a joy, and the winters, although a little cold, are short.

It is such a beautiful place, and the crops grow so well, that there is little for the Farian people to do but enjoy themselves in the sun. So they rarely work, and instead, spend their days playing, having parties, making music, and telling each other wonderful stories.

Some people might say that they are lazy. But they wouldn't care, because they are just so happy.

But one year it wasn't like that. That year, in fact, the people of Faria were far from happy. Indeed, they were very worried, for although spring should have arrived weeks before—it hadn't. None of the winter snows were gone yet, the lakes had not thawed, the birds were not building their nests, and the buds of the flowers in the mountain meadows had failed to open.

"It's not good enough!" said the king. "Something must be done."

He summoned the members of his Great Council to meet at the palace. "What can be wrong?" he asked them. "What has happened to the spring?"

All the men and women of the Great Council, except for one, shook their heads, for they did not know the answer. But the oldest and wisest member stood up.

"It is because the Spring Unicorn, the bringer of spring, has not visited Faria this year," he explained. "Without his arrival, there can be no spring."

The king and the other members of the council looked at each other and frowned.

"But why has the Spring Unicorn not come to Faria?" asked the king. "Doesn't he like us anymore?"

"I think it could be because we are so busy enjoying ourselves that we never thank the Spring Unicorn for all he does for us. It could be that he thinks we are lazy and don't deserve to live in such a wonderful place," suggested the wisest council member.

"But we must put that right at once," said the king. "All the people in all the land must leave the warmth of their homes and go out and start work immediately. They must start, ummmm, they must, ummmm…"

The king wanted to describe the sort of things his people should be doing when they went out to work—but the trouble was he knew nothing about work, so he didn't know what to say. Finally, he just said, "Er… they must, you know, they must bustle about being busy, doing work and things."

So, because the king told them to, the people of Faria
went to work. At first, they didn't even know what to do.
Then, when they'd looked up the word in the Faria
dictionary, and found out what was involved, they
didn't like the sound of it, and grumbled a
lot among themselves.

But, as time passed,
they discovered that they actually
enjoyed being busy. They shoveled the snow from
the paths of their gardens, they cleared snow from the
roads, they repaired leaking roofs, and even filled all the
holes in the roads. And they still laughed and sang, the way
they used to before the spring failed to arrive and the king
ordered them all to go to work.

But it still kept snowing, the lakes didn't thaw, the birds failed to build their nests, and the flowers didn't bloom.

"What can the matter be now?" the king asked the oldest and wisest member of his council.

"Perhaps the Spring Unicorn doesn't know how hard we've been working," said the wise man.

"Well, the Spring Unicorn must be told," snapped the king, stamping his royal foot.

That very day, messengers were sent throughout the land to put up posters announcing that anyone who found the Spring Unicorn and explained how hard the Farians had been working would receive all the gold they could wish for.

The problem was that nobody knew where the Spring Unicorn lived, and nobody felt brave enough to go out and look for him. Nobody, that was, except for a poor musician who was known as The Whistler.

"I'm fed up with winter, and I've got nothing better to do, so I might just as well go and look for the Spring Unicorn," thought The Whistler.

So he picked up his flute and set off in search of the Spring Unicorn. He traveled far and wide, playing his flute to keep him cheerful on his journey. And as he played, the notes of the flute danced before him, leading him on and on, across the widest oceans, over the highest mountains.

"I shall follow the notes of my music wherever they lead me," he told himself.

At long last, he came to a valley where no one had ever been before. It was the home of the Spring Unicorn.

"You have no place here," boomed a loud voice. "How did you, a mere Farian, find your way here?"

"I played my flute and followed the notes," explained The Whistler. Then he demonstrated with a quick tune.

His music was so beautiful that within minutes a whole herd of magical unicorns appeared and danced before him.

When he finally laid down his flute, one of the unicorns trotted forward. He introduced himself as the Spring Unicorn.

"Why are you here?" the Spring Unicorn asked.

"Because you failed to come to Faria this year," explained The Whistler.

"Ha!" cried the Spring Unicorn. "I couldn't be bothered to come, because the people of Faria are so lazy they do not deserve my beautiful springs."

"But what you say is no longer true," explained The Whistler. "We are no longer lazy. And we still have time to be happy, telling each other wonderful tales and playing beautiful music while we work."

With that, he picked up his flute again and began to play the sweetest tune the Spring Unicorn had ever heard.

"Maybe you are right," said the Spring Unicorn, when the tune had come to an end. "I'll tell you what I'll do. Providing you play your beautiful music on your journey back to Faria, I shall accompany you, and we will see if the people there are no longer lazy."

"Can I fly on your back?" asked The Whistler hopefully.

"No," said the Spring Unicorn. "If we fly, the journey will be over too quickly, and I won't have time to listen to all the music I want you to play. We shall walk back the way you came."

"Oh, drat," thought The Whistler, whose legs were really aching from all the miles he had walked on his journey to find the Spring Unicorn. Even so, he agreed to do as the Spring Unicorn asked.

So The Whistler returned the way he had come. And throughout his long journey he played the most beautiful music, so that the Spring Unicorn followed every step of the way.

Eventually they arrived in the mountains above Faria.

"Look," said The Whistler, pointing down to the village. "See how hard the people are working."

And indeed they were. Some were shoveling snow from their gardens—but as soon as they had finished, more snow fell to replace it. Some were clearing snow from the roads—but as soon as they stood up to rest their backs, more snow covered them. Some were fixing leaks in their roofs—but as soon as they finished, more snow fell to make new holes.

"Indeed, they are working," admitted the Spring Unicorn. "But are they happy in their work?"

"Listen," said The Whistler.

The Unicorn listened. Faintly, from the village, came the sound of someone laughing. Someone else was whistling. Someone else was singing.

"Oh, yes," said The Whistler. "I think you can say they are happy."

"I believe you're right," agreed the Unicorn. "You shall have your spring back again, and I shall continue to bring a new spring, year after year, just as long as the people remain happy and contented and do not ever become lazy again."

That's how it was. And that's how it still is. Spring comes every year to Faria, and the people remain happy and contented. They work harder now than they did before, but never too hard. There is still time for them to party and make music and tell each other stories.

And The Whistler? Well, he turned down the king's offer of riches in favor of becoming the Spring Unicorn's helper. Which is why, every year, the Farian spring is always heralded by the most beautiful music anyone has ever heard.

Floyd, the Friendly Shark

Deep beneath the ocean blue, there lived a young shark called Floyd. Now, Floyd might have looked like other young sharks, but beneath his hard skin, he was a big softy.

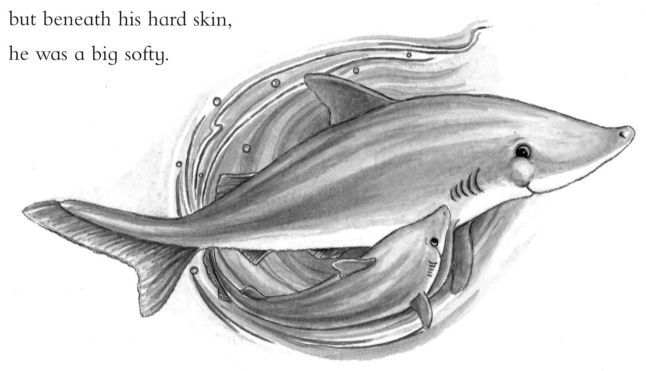

It had begun when he was a baby. While the other young sharks were swimming around fearlessly, Floyd had stuck to his mother's side.

"Don't be such a limpet!" she'd whisper, trying to ignore the other shark mothers, who giggled as they swam by.

Things didn't improve when Floyd went to school. All the other sharks seemed so rough and unfriendly, and when recess came, he always found himself alone.

"Why can't I play with some of the other sea animals, Mother?" he asked.

"Floyd, you're a shark," said his mother gently. "Sharks play with other sharks. I don't want to see you hanging around with any old octopus or eel. The other sharks would just tease you."

Floyd felt sad. He would have loved to make friends with the octopuses, who could play four different ball games at once. Or the

eels, who seemed to have so much fun using each other as jump ropes.

It wasn't as if he hadn't tried, either.

Once, he'd swum past some
young squids who were having
a wonderful time squirting
each other with ink.

"Hi!" Floyd said hopefully,
flashing his wide, toothy smile.

"Ahhh!" shrieked the squids. They
squirted ink in Floyd's face before
propelling themselves away
as fast as their
tentacles
could
carry
them.

A very inky
Floyd had swum
sadly away.

Wherever he went, it was the
same story. At the sight of his big toothy
grin, all the sea animals fled to the
safety of their caves and crevices,
and hid behind their mothers.
So Floyd spent most of his
days swimming around alone.

One day, while Floyd was exploring some rocks near the beach, something caught his eye. A large blue dolphin was tangled up in a net and was thrashing around, trying to get free.

When he saw Floyd, the dolphin thrashed even harder. He turned an alarmed eye in Floyd's direction.

"Don't bite me!" he pleaded.

"I have no intention of biting you," said Floyd in an upset voice. "I just came over to see if you needed any help."

The dolphin looked at Floyd's sharp teeth and gulped. But then he noticed Floyd's gentle eyes. Anyone with eyes as kind as that couldn't be too dangerous.

"You could try making a hole in this net," suggested the dolphin timidly. "It shouldn't be too difficult, with teeth like yours." Floyd chomped through the net in no time, and the dolphin wriggled free.

"Thanks," cried the dolphin, before flipping his tail and darting away.

Floyd followed him and watched in
admiration as he swam gracefully to the surface
and leaped high out of the water.

Later, as they swam along, the dolphin told Floyd how he
entertained the people at the beach by jumping through hoops and
giving them rides.

"I could do that!" thought Floyd, as he followed the dolphin to the
shore. His eyes crinkled in a happy smile as he pictured the children's
faces as he carried them around on his back, or entertained them with
amazing backflips!

It was a hot day, and the shore was crowded with bathers.

"Here goes," thought Floyd, as he popped his head out
of the water. "Who'll be the first to have a ride?"

But nobody seemed to want a ride.

In fact, judging by all the running and screaming, it seemed that the last thing that anyone wanted was to go anywhere near Floyd.

"Go back, Floyd!" called the dolphin. "Don't you know that people are terrified of sharks?"

So once again, the friendless little shark swam sadly away. "It doesn't look like I'll ever have any real friends," he sniffed sadly. "I might as well get used to being all alone." He dived back beneath the ocean and swam round and round.

He was far out at sea when he heard a cry for help. He looked up, and made out the shape of an air mattress floating above him on top of the water.

Nervously, he raised his head above the surface. He found himself eye to eye with a small girl.

"Are you a s...s...shark?" stuttered the girl in terror.

She had been told to steer clear of sharks.

"Don't worry," Floyd said hastily, seeing the fear in her eyes. "I won't hurt you. I'm a friendly shark."

Floyd gave her a small, hopeful smile. It was a somewhat strange smile, since he was doing his best to keep his teeth out of sight, but it seemed to reassure the little girl. She reached out and stroked his back. "Oooh," she giggled, "your skin's all rough!"

"What on earth are you doing so far from the shore?" asked Floyd.

"I drifted out," the little girl said sadly. "Mom's always telling me not to, but I forgot. She's going to be furious," she added gloomily.

"Hang on," said Floyd. He dived down and grabbed a piece of the net that had trapped the dolphin. "Here you are," he said. "Sling this around my neck, and hold on tight!"

Remembering the fuss he had caused earlier, Floyd kept well below the water until he had pulled the little girl to shore. Only when she was safely in the arms of her father did he pop his head above the water. He bared his teeth and gave his terrifying smile.

"It's a shark," said the little girl's mother faintly. She looked at Floyd and the net that still hung around his neck. "Our daughter's been saved by a shark."

After that, Floyd was the toast of the beach. He gave rides to children and raced his friend the dolphin back and forth across the bay to his heart's content. Sometimes the other sharks would tease him for being such a friendly shark, but Floyd didn't mind—he had more friends than any other shark in the ocean!

As for Floyd's mother—well, she couldn't help boasting about her son. After all, he wasn't like other sharks. He was much nicer!

Little Red Riding Hood

Once upon a time, there was a little girl who lived with her mother in a tiny cottage on the edge of a large forest. The little girl's grandmother had made her a beautiful red cloak with a hood, so people called her Little Red Riding Hood.

One day, Little Red Riding Hood's mother asked her to take a basket of food to her grandmother, who wasn't very well. She lived on the other side of the woods. It was a lovely day, and Little Red Riding Hood always enjoyed visiting Granny, so she waved happily to her mother and skipped away.

Little Red Riding Hood hadn't skipped very far when she stopped to pick some flowers for her grandmother. Just then a crafty-looking wolf wandered by.

"Hellooo, my lovely!" he smiled. "Where are you going on this fine day?"

"I'm going to see Granny, who lives in the cottage on the other side of the woods," explained Little Red Riding Hood, who had not been told never to speak to strangers. "She's not very well, so I'm taking her this basket of food and a bunch of flowers."

"What a thoughtful girl," purred the wolf, trying to hide his sly grin. "Well, I must dash. See you!"

"Seems like a nice wolf, although he does appear to be in kind of a rush," thought Little Red Riding Hood as she watched him race away. But then she forgot all about the wolf and skipped on through the woods.

Meanwhile, the wolf, who wasn't nice at all, ran all the way to

Little Red Riding Hood's grandmother's house. "Oh, goody," he smiled, as he peeked through the window and saw Granny lying in bed. "It's almost too easy." He licked his lips and rubbed his rumbling tummy.

"Yoo-hoo!" he called, as he knocked on the door.

"Is that you, Little Red Riding Hood?" croaked Granny, who had a sore throat. "Come in, the door's open. I've been expecting you."

With that, the wicked wolf pushed his way into the cottage and gobbled up Granny in a single gulp. Then, quick as a flash, he put on her spare nightgown and nightcap, put on her glasses, and jumped into her bed.

A few minutes later, when Little Red Riding Hood knocked on the door, the wolf pulled the blankets up to his chin. "Come in, my dear," he called, in his very best grandmother voice. "The door is open."

Little Red Riding Hood skipped into the house. "I've brought you some yummy food, and…" Little Red Riding Hood stopped in her tracks when she caught sight of her grandmother.

"Oh dear, Granny, what big eyes you have," she said, feeling just the tiniest bit afraid.

"All the better to see you with, my dear," replied the sneaky wolf.

"But Granny, what big ears you have," she whispered, beginning to feel very afraid.

"All the better to hear you with, my dear," replied the wolf, trying not to snicker.

"And Granny, what big teeth you have," she squeaked, now feeling absolutely terrified. "All the better to EAT you with," roared the wolf, as he leaped from the bed.

Little Red Riding Hood managed one ear-piercing scream before the wolf pounced and gobbled her up in a single gulp.

Out in the forest, a passing woodcutter heard the loud scream and raced to see what was happening. He charged into the cottage, where the greedy wolf was smacking his lips with glee. Quick as a flash, the woodcutter swung his ax and killed the wolf with a single blow. Then he drew out his knife and slit open the wolf's bulging belly.

Out popped Little Red Riding Hood and her grandmother. Granny was so pleased that she invited the woodcutter to tea.

From that day on, Little Red Riding Hood never talked to strangers again—especially ones with big eyes, big ears, and big teeth!